Visit us at www.boldstrokesbooks.com

By the Author

Share the Moon

The Marriage Masquerade

Gia's Gems

GIA'S GEMS

by
Toni Logan

2021

GIA'S GEMS

ISBN 13: 978-1-63555-917-0

This Trade Paperback Original Is Published By
Bold Strokes Books, Inc.
P.O. Box 249
Valley Falls, NY 12185

First Edition: November 2021

CREDITS
EDITOR: BARBARA ANN WRIGHT
PRODUCTION DESIGN: SUSAN RAMUNDO
COVER DESIGN BY TAMMY SEIDICK

Acknowledgments

A heartfelt thank you to Radclyffe, Sandy, and the incredible team at Bold Strokes Books. I am honored and forever grateful to be a part of this amazing family. Thank you.

A very special shoutout to Barbara Ann Wright, editor extraordinaire, for your patience and guidance. I definitely owe you a huge box of goodies.

For my wonderful friends, I thank you for always being there for me. You guys keep me smiling. I love you.

To Tammy, for sharing all the crazy stories of her cat, Brody, and to Ronnie for the late night text messages of encouragement and comments about all things writing.

And the biggest thank you goes to you, the reader, for taking a chance on this book. I hope you enjoy reading it as much as I enjoyed writing it.

Dedication

To Evelyn Bean (Beaner)

PROLOGUE

"Did you get the pics I sent you?" Stacy said in an over amplified voice.

"Where are you right now? I hear loud music." Gia Williams clutched a glass of merlot, sank into the well-worn spot on her couch, and put her bare feet up. She hit the speaker button, and scrolled through Stacy's latest pictures of food, scenery, and selfie pictures.

"I'm at a bar sampling the local brew that the bartender said was halfway decent. And he was right, it's not bad."

"Beer? Thought you were on a wine kick?" Gia turned her phone sideways and smiled at a cute selfie of Stacy standing in front of an old stone building with the sign Brillow's Brewery in the background.

"That was last week. Besides, I'm at some hole-in-the-wall beer bar that's south of Chicago, as in *way* south of Chicago, and believe it or not, this place is like a gay mecca. I mean, seriously, how can there be so many of us living in such a tiny little…Oh. My. God."

"What?" Gia stopped looking at the photos and gave Stacy her undivided attention.

"There's a gorgeous Amazon woman at the end of the bar, totally staring me down right now, and I kid you not, she just licked her lips."

"Wow, someone's going to get lucky tonight," Gia replied in a half-hearted way. Stacy always got lucky, so the fact that someone was licking their lips at her wasn't a news flash.

"I don't know. My kinky meter is starting to ping. She reminds me of someone I hooked up with in Atlanta, and holy hell, that woman had an arsenal of crazy ass toys that would make most lesbians blush. I'm not sure I'm in the mood for that kind of thing tonight," Stacy said.

"Well, it's a good thing you're not like most lesbians," Gia said as she returned her attention to the photos. She already knew that if something was pinging Stacy's meter that much, it was a lure she wouldn't be able to resist. "Take a picture of her and send it to me," Gia said as she flicked her thumb and first finger across the screen of her phone and enlarged a selfie of Stacy biting into a rather large, mysterious looking pastry.

"I have a better idea, why don't you start getting your ass out of your house and back into the world so you can send *me* pictures of *your* dysfunctional one-nighters with eccentric women?"

Gia rolled her eyes and downed half her glass of wine. Here they went again, the never-ending prodding to get her out of her self-induced home coma and back into the land of the living. "You know why, Stacy." Gia sighed. "I'm just not ready yet, and besides, you know I'm agoraphobic."

Stacy snorted. "You're not agoraphobic, you have bruised ego-itis, and will you please stay off those self-diagnose websites? Remember what happened last time? You about scared the shit out of me when you called crying hysterically because you thought the spot on your thigh was cancer when it was really—"

"I know, I know," Gia interrupted. "Just dried chocolate. But this is different."

"No, Gia, it isn't. Stop looking outside yourself for excuses and start looking within for answers. It's going on two years. Don't you think that's long enough?" Stacy huffed.

"Hey, according to all the inspirational sites on my social feed, it'll take as long as it takes." Okay, maybe Stacy was right. But damn it, she was still in pain after being dumped and Stacy knew that. So what if she had spent the last two years not wanting to go out in public or date anyone? She didn't have to. All the wonderful convivences of technology both satisfied and enabled her antisocial mood. She telecommuted, shopped online, had food delivered to her house, streamed movies, attended video conferencing calls for work, and fired up her vibrator when the mood hit. It was a self-diagnosed agoraphobic's wet dream, and for right now, it was exactly what she thought she needed to heal.

"Uh-oh," Stacy mumbled.

"What? What's going on? Give me the play-by-play." Gia finished off the remainder of her wine and anxiously waited for her reply. Living vicariously through her best friend had become her only attachment to the outside world, and she relished in Stacy's descriptive narrative.

"The Amazon queen just sent me a beer," Stacy said in a low voice.

"You already have a beer."

"I know, I guess she wants me good and drunk tonight."

"On two beers?" Gia chuckled as she settled deeper into the couch cushion, knowing full well that Stacy could drink most people under the table.

"Well, two's a good start for the kind of night I think this woman has in mind," Stacy said.

"Ew. That's a little more information than…ouch." Gia gently slapped at her cat Brody, who sat on top of the cushion behind her.

"Ouch what? Ouch for me getting some tonight with an Amazon woman?" Stacy asked.

"No, ouch for me. Brody is sitting behind me using my head as a kneading pad. Which is reminding me that I really need to trim his claws."

"You do know that a beautiful woman could be doing that to you."

"Clawing my head?" Gia grunted.

"No. Massaging you. Some hot babe could be running her fingers through your hair right now."

Gia leaned forward and out of Brody's reach. She caught her reflection in the mirror on the opposite wall, and thanks to Brody, the left side of her head looked like it had been caught in a wind tunnel. She gently peeled the feline off the top of the cushion and placed him by her lap. "I think I'll pass." As much as she would love feeling the touch of a woman on any part of her body, she did not welcome the drama and bullshit that came with that package. "No, thanks," she mumbled to herself as she blew at the strands of her hair tickling across her face. She undid her hair tie and placed it in her mouth as she palmed her hair behind her head.

"Shit. Shit. Shit," Stacy barked into the phone.

"What?" Gia shoved her hair into the elastic band.

"Amazon woman approaching, gotta go."

"Practice safe sex." Gia quickly threw out in a teasing way, but the connection had already gone dead. "Guess Stacy's in for another fun night, huh, big boy?" She ran her fingers down Brody's back as he climbed on her bare leg and began kneading. "Ouch, ouch. Enough already." Red, needle-like marks appeared on her skin. She gently scooped him off her leg and placed him back on the cushion next to her. She had to repeat that action three more times before he finally gave up and curled in a ball.

As she sat back and finished scrolling through the remainder of Stacy's pictures, a pang of jealousy hit her. Stacy was out embracing life while she hid from it. She stared at the last picture in the sequence and found herself being drawn into the quaintness of Stacy's recent small-town adventures. Good ol' Stace, she thought. She gets to go to some of the weirdest and most interesting places.

Stacy worked for a mid-sized tech company that developed a medical software app that helped track a patient from admission to release and all things in between. The added bonus for the hospitals and clinics that signed up for the software was that she flew to their facility for a two-day, hands-on training session. It was a perk that brought Stacy to small towns in places Gia never heard of or knew existed. And with Stacy's extroverted personality and excellent gaydar, it didn't take her long to sniff out anything or anyone who even remotely hinted of gayness. The stories she relayed of her escapades were entertainingly colorful, and just as she had done since the time when they were teens, she hung on every descriptive word.

They had been swapping stories about women, love, and life since high school. Fast forward twenty years, and the only thing that Gia thought had changed between then and now was their age. Well, that and the fact that neither of their lives looked anything like they thought it would. Who knew being rich, successful, and in a long-term relationship was so hard to obtain?

As she studied Stacy's photos through the intoxicating fog now hovering around her brain, she could almost see herself as the one taking the pictures. "All right, Stacy," she said as she forwarded the photos to her email account. "Since you think it's time for me to have a life, I'll have yours." She stumbled into her bedroom and returned with her laptop. She settled back on the couch, opened the computer and activated her photo editing software. She picked eight of what she considered were the best of Stacy's pictures and one by one, began photoshopping herself into the scenes.

She created a three-page article on *her* adventures as a single, thirty-something lesbian traveling around to small towns and finding the little gay gems each had to offer. She took the information Stacy told her about her latest travel escapades and embellished them. She focused on the food, the idiosyncrasies, the nuances, and the hidden away places and spaces that Stacy seemed to have an uncanny way of sniffing out. As Gia poured herself more wine, she poured her wit into the humorous and informative fictitious piece.

By the time she looked up from her computer and glanced at the clock, it was two in the morning. She arched her back, stretched and looked down at Brody. "What should we call this masterpiece, huh, big boy?" Brody didn't look up, as though he couldn't be bothered to acknowledge any human sentence that didn't have the words *din-din time* in it. "How about…" She cocked her head as she typed *Gia's Gems* at the top. "There, take that, Stacy." She yawned as she hit send. She placed the computer on the coffee table, stood, and turned to Brody. "I'm heading to bed, you coming?" Brody didn't stir. "Fine." She headed to her bedroom, knowing he had not only heard the word bed, but by the time she peed and brushed her teeth, he would be curled up in the middle of her pillow. Gia smiled. So what if she was a self-induced weirdo right now? At least she didn't have any drama in her life. Well, to be fair, she really didn't have anything in her life except her job, Stacy, and her cat. But hey, she was content. And content was so much better than what she had been.

❖

Stacy's body was aching. With her limited knowledge of the human anatomy, she didn't even think she had muscles in some of the places that were now throbbing.

"What a night." She chuckled to herself as she hobbled into the hotel's coffeeshop with her suitcase in tow. The sign at the empty hostess stand instructed her to seat herself, so she picked the first empty booth.

A server carrying a menu and carafe of coffee approached. She mouthed a thank you as the server poured a cup. She took a sip and cringed. She had tasted some pretty nasty coffee in her travels, but she was always grateful for the end result. "If you have a veggie omelet with hashbrowns, I'll have that."

The server nodded as she scribbled the order on a small notepad, turned, and headed for the kitchen. Stacy relaxed against the back cushion of the booth and, feeling as though she was finally back amongst the land of the living, dug in her purse and pulled out her phone. She had a plane to catch in four hours, and she wanted to make sure it was on time. As she activated her screen, she noticed her email icon indicated she already had ten. "How is that even possible?" She groaned. "It's not even six o'clock." As she debated which she should open first, her eyes wandered to the last on the list. It was from Gia, timestamped at two in the morning. "Do you ever sleep?" she mumbled as she tapped it open. But who was she to talk? By two in the morning, she was on her second rodeo ride around a toy she never knew existed.

As she topped off her coffee, she began reading. A professionally designed, two-page story, peppered with Gia's photoshopped pictures, stared back at her. "What the hell?" Within minutes, she was laughing as she read Gia's comical spin on her own words, turning them into a charming adventure. "Damn, girl, you still got it," she said as the server placed the food in front of her.

Stacy finished Gia's article, but before she closed the email, a thought crossed her mind. She hit the forward arrow and typed in the address of a friend who was the assistant to the senior editor at the popular lesbian online magazine, *L Online*.

Hey, Sara,

You remember me telling you about my friend Gia? Well, I thought I would pass along a sample of her writing. Just in case anything opens up at L.

Hope you're doing well.

Stacy

She hoped after *L Online* read Gia's article, they might hire her to do some freelance writing, and maybe in turn, that would help Gia emerge from her cocoon. She hit send, placed her phone back in her purse, and grabbed the salt shaker. By this afternoon, she would be in another town, working with another clinic, and hopefully, enjoying another round of local hospitality. And maybe—she arched her aching back and rolled her sore shoulders—she could book a massage for later that evening.

For a brief moment, she wondered if she was getting too old for late night hook-ups. "Nah." She smiled as she slid her fork into the greasy omelet and replayed a scene from the previous night. As long as her libido was still firing on all cylinders, she was in it for the ride. And she was really enjoying the ride.

❖

"What do you mean, they want to publish it? How did they even get it?" Gia didn't know if she should feel flattered that *L Online* wanted to publish her work or pissed at what Stacy did.

"I might have sent it to my friend Sara over there. She's the assistant to the senior editor, who might have showed it to her boss."

"That's an awful lot of *might haves*." Gia cradled her phone between her cheek and shoulder, while she opened a can of wet cat food. "Din-din time," she said as Brody let out an ear-piercing yowl.

"What the hell was that?"

"That was Brody." Gia giggled. "You'd think wet food smelled like a female in heat." She dumped the contents on a small plate and placed it on the floor. "There you go, sweetie."

"Anyway, I didn't mean for them to want to publish the actual article. I just thought I would send it in as a sample of your writing. But it doesn't surprise me that they fell in love with it. It's a well-written and entertaining piece, Gia."

"But it's not real. I didn't do any of those things. You did." She leaned against her counter and pinched the bridge of her nose. Again, she was flattered beyond words for the offer to publish, but her stomach soured as she wondered if the article teetered on the edge of plagiarism.

"Yeah, but they don't know that," Stacy said.

"But I only wrote it as a joke for you." Gia huffed.

"I know, but it's good, Gia, really good. And besides, you've always wanted to be a writer and get out from under your corporate job. Maybe this is your opportunity."

"But it's a lie."

"Then just let them publish it this one time and let it go at that. This way, you'll be able to say you're a published writer. One and done and no one will be the wiser. What could it possibly hurt?"

What could it possibly hurt? The question echoed in her head. She had always dreamed of being a published writer, and here was her chance. True, it was Stacy's adventures and pictures, but it was her words, and that was what really mattered. She rubbed her neck as she weighed the decision. But in the end, her desire to be published overruled her better judgment. Besides, it wasn't like anyone was ever going to find out.

CHAPTER ONE

Three years later

"Sara called from *L*. They're renewing my contract for another two years." Gia pressed the phone against her ear. She was enjoying the success and growing fanbase from her column in *L Online*, and the exposure had recently led to three mainstream travel magazines requesting content.

"Well, I'm not surprised. You have quite the following," Stacy said.

"I know, kinda crazy when I think about it." Last year, she was able to quit her day job when the money coming in from her writing was enough to maintain her lifestyle. She was finally living her dream, and she couldn't be happier. "What are you doing?" She could hear Stacy moving around and softly groaning. "Oh God, please tell me you're not having sex while you're talking to me."

"No, I'm not having sex, so you can put away your voyeur fantasy. I'm actually trying to pack, but I don't really have anything to wear, and it's frustrating."

"You have your master and spare bedroom closets stuffed with clothes and shoes, and you're telling me you have nothing to wear?" Gia teased.

"I know, I can't help it. I'm an embarrassment to minimalists everywhere," Stacy said. "But I'm off to some small town on the outskirts of Seattle, so I'll need to bring enough to layer."

"Send tons of pics. It'll be my next *Gia's Gems* travel."

"Gia." Stacy exhaled, and Gia instantly tensed. She knew that tone well, and she also knew the words that would follow. "How long you gonna keep this up?"

"I know, I know. I'm getting there. I just need..." She searched for the right words. "A little more time." But she knew that wasn't totally true. She has had plenty of time. Five years of it to be exact, and the only thing that had changed between then and now was her becoming more isolated not less. No, what she needed was something all-together different. Something that would jolt her out of her comatose lifestyle. If that was even possible.

"You know, sooner or later, someone's going to find out about what we're doing, and it isn't going to end well."

"Well, I'll cross that bridge when I come to it." Even though Gia had been hesitant to go along with the scheme at first, she was now the driving force that kept it going. She had become neck deep in the lie and was enjoying everything it had to offer.

"Sweetie, it's been over five years since you've led a normal life, and don't get huffy, I'm putting the word *normal* in air quotes. Look, all I'm saying is that maybe it's time to venture outside your little bubble and reclaim your life. This isn't healthy, and I'm more than a little worried about you."

Gia could feel the anxiety surge through her. She knew Stacy was right, but damn it, she had created a comfortable and safe life in her little rabbit hole. Her therapist was online, and her morning yoga class was delivered to her living room every morning, courtesy of YouTube. She'd hired a college student to run her errands, and all aspects of *Gia's Gems* were easily handled through phone calls, texts, and digital transfers. As unhealthy as that was, it was easy, convenient, and it had become her routine. And routines, no matter how abnormal they might seem to everyone else, felt very normal to those living them. Besides, her life could be a hell of a lot worse. At least in *this* rabbit hole, she wouldn't get her heart broken and smashed into tiny irreparable pieces. "Don't worry, I'm fine. Besides, my therapist said I'm making great strides."

"Your therapist is a joke." Stacy scoffed.

"Maybe. But she's hot as hell."

"You do know there are websites out there where you can watch hot women all day long, and they charge half of what your therapist charges."

Gia remained silent. She knew she wasn't making any gains with her therapist, but that didn't bother her. The sessions were easy, she was never pushed into talking about anything uncomfortable, and the woman really was stunningly gorgeous. She didn't care if she gave her more money than she was probably worth. Life was good, she lived in a comfortable bubble, and nothing was forcing her to change. Sometimes, the status quo worked just fine.

"Look." Stacy continued. "Just promise me when I return from this trip, you'll start getting serious about getting your life back."

"All right, all right. I'll think about it. Meanwhile, go be adventurous for me, so I can write vicariously through you."

"You know I love you." Stacy threw out.

"I love you too, Stace. Now, go bring me back some fun stories." Gia hung up and tossed her phone on the coffee table. She reached for her tablet and opened up *L Online*. She scrolled through the feature article about another B-list Hollywood lesbian celebrity who just came out, until she settled on page seven. *Gia's Gems* page. There, staring back at her from the top corner of the article, was her author photo. It was the only real picture of her in the entire piece. She was standing on the edge of a cliff in Maui, overlooking the ocean. It had been taken during happier times, when she and Audrey were at the beginning of their five-year relationship. When Gia had felt like her world was so much more predictable. Funny how the sudden turn of a card had changed her life so completely. No, scratch that. It hadn't changed her life; it had changed *her*. "I guess I really am a mess," she mumbled as she turned to Brody. "And pathetic." She raked her fingers down his back. "Maybe Stacy's right?" She began scratching under his chin. Maybe it was time to get back out into the world. But how was she going to crawl out of a hole that she'd spent the past five years of her life digging? And such a comfortable hole at that.

CHAPTER TWO

L indsey Callahan pushed the button that lowered the driver side window. She'd inherited the white Dodge minivan when her mother passed away a few months ago, and driving it felt like a part of her mom was still with her. She rested her left arm on the door and breathed in the morning. It was another beautiful summer day in Jacobe, Missouri, and as usual, Lindsey was in a good mood. She sang to her favorite radio station as she drove the ten minutes from her house to Frieda's, the small restaurant off Main Street.

She parked in front and cut the engine. She looked around for her best friend Jenn, but didn't see any sign of her. "Sweet," she whispered as she dug in her backpack, pulled out her tablet, and tapped the *L Online* app. She scrolled passed the opening articles and went right to page seven. She was a huge fan of *Gia's Gems* and harbored a serious crush on the woman in the author's photo overlooking the ocean. "What a fun gig," she said to herself as she sat back in her seat. The sun felt warm and welcoming on her skin, and she blocked out everything around her as she focused on the article.

"Hey," Jenn said in a loud voice.

Lindsey startled. "Jeezus, you scared the shit out of me."

"Well, then, stop looking at porn. And oh my God, what attacked your hair?"

"The wind." Lindsey shoved her tablet in her backpack and hopped out. She checked herself in the side mirror and pulled at sections of her hair.

"Oh, for fuck's sake. You're making it worse. Come here." Jenn turned and expertly moved her fingers around Lindsey's head.

Lindsey playfully slapped at her hand. "I got it, I got it."

Jenn slapped back. "No, you don't, and you do realize we're in public. Stand still." Jenn twisted and smoothed Lindsey's hair until she had it back to looking fashionably messy. "There, now I'm not as embarrassed to be with you."

"Says the woman who was so drunk one night, she was tossing scraps of pizza to a basketball in the park while loudly saying, here, kitty-kitty," Lindsey reminded her.

"Who knew an out-of-focus basketball looked so much like a fluffy tabby cat? And besides, that was *before* I realized how much I needed glasses."

"No, that was *after* you had close to four glasses of wine, and for the record, basketballs don't look anything like a cat." Jenn's latest drinking binge had come on the heels of a nasty breakup. Unfortunately, it had also come on the heels of Lindsey's mother's passing. As much as she wanted to be emotionally available for Jenn during that time, she was so tapped out, all she could offer was a shoulder to cry on. But maybe that was all Jenn needed. "Come on, I'm starving." She flung her backpack over her shoulder and walked inside.

"Hey, Lindsey. Hey, Jenn," a bubbly teenager with pink-streaked hair greeted them as she grabbed two menus.

"Hi, Vanessa, how are you this morning?" Lindsey asked as she was escorted to their usual booth in the back against a window.

"Can't complain." Vanessa placed the menus on the table as they slid into opposite bench seats. "Two coffees, one with almond milk, the other black, right?"

"You got it," Jenn answered as she leaned back and folded her arms. "What were you really looking at in the car?"

Lindsey pulled out her tablet and opened up *L*'s latest issue. "I was just starting to read *Gia's Gems*." As always, the thought of Gia made her smile. Yes, she was attracted to her, but it wasn't just physical. Gia represented something she had lost a long time ago and had yet to get back. It was the desire to be spontaneous and free to just pick up and go whenever the mood hit. What she would have once given to have that opportunity.

"Oh yeah, where's she this time?" Jenn asked.

"Somewhere in Colorado, but I didn't get too far because someone interrupted me." Lindsey cleared her throat.

"Sure you weren't looking at her picture more than her words?" Jenn teased.

"That sounds so pathetically desperate." Lindsey sighed. Was that what she had become? So pathetic that she identified with a stranger's life more than her own?

"You guys ready to order?" Vanessa asked as she placed two large colorful mugs in front of them.

Jenn nodded. "We'll have our usual."

"Sounds good," Vanessa said as she collected the menus.

"Is Jackie not doing it for you?" Jenn poured sugar into her mug, grabbed a spoon, and gently stirred.

"It's not that. I mean, I like Jackie. She's nice and all, but—"

"You do know," Jenn interrupted. "When you call the woman you've been on a couple dates with *nice*, it's really code for *I'm just not into her*."

Lindsey shrugged. "Yeah, I guess I'm just not into her." She'd met Jackie at the bar late one night after she'd bought her a drink. Jackie lived one town over, was a fresh face in a sea of locals, and was easy to talk to. By the end of the evening, they were making plans to go on a date, and maybe a wonderful relationship would follow. But after a sparkless good night kiss, she pumped the brakes on those thoughts. No sense moving in that direction when there just wasn't anything there.

"Well, maybe you can be friends?" Jenn threw out.

"Sure. I'll add her to my ever growing"—Lindsey frowned as she made air quotes—"friends list." She took a sip of coffee to help wash away a feeling of loneliness that was settling in. "Oh wow, that tastes good. Frieda definitely upped her coffee game."

"I hear she's dating the supplier." Jenn leaned in as she spilled the latest gossip.

"Who told you that?" Lindsey asked.

"The grapevine," Jenn said a bit sarcastically. "How else does news travel around this town?"

"True." Lindsey nodded. Jacobe's grapevine was amazing at gathering and dispersing information. But as much as she was in awe at the speed at which a story could fly around the town, she knew firsthand how much slower that same information moved when it needed to be corrected.

Jenn sipped her coffee. "Damn, this really is good." She smacked her lips a couple of times. "So how're things going with the estate?"

Lindsey shrugged. *Estate* seemed like such a big word to refer to what was left of her parents' meager lives. Her dad had been a school teacher, and her mom had worked at the local hardware store. When Lindsey came along as an unplanned pregnancy later in their lives, the income dropped to one. And in the end, all that was left of an inheritance was a century-old house and high-mileage minivan—both paid for—a couple life insurance policies, and a depleted savings account. "I should get the last insurance check next week."

"Please tell me you're finally going to get out of this town and treat yourself to a real vacation?"

Lindsey shook her head. "No. I need to spend the money on all the repairs around the house that I put off while mom was still alive." She calculated that after the renovations—and if she remained as frugal as her parents once were—she would have enough to live on for the next couple of years. Maybe by then, she could figure out what the next chapter of her life looked like.

"No. What you *need* is a vacation." Jenn stabbed a finger at her.

When she was young, Lindsey hadn't cared that her family never had the means to indulge in anything more than a local outing. But as she'd gotten older and listened to her classmates talk about their summer vacations in other states and parts of the world, she'd become envious. When she'd quizzed her parents on why they never ventured out of state, she was told all the money they would be spending on travel was going into her college fund. A small sacrifice to make, they'd said, for a future that would pay dividends. Unfortunately, it was a future that she had never been able to cash in on.

"So, Linds," Jenn said as Vanessa placed two large plates in front of them. "You're going to join us tonight, right?"

"Tell me again which one of your exes is coming to town." Lindsey grabbed her fork and thought about the last time she'd agreed to meet up with Jenn and another woman. She'd gone from feeling comfortable to awkward when it had become clear she was the third person in what had become a two-person play. She was not anxious to put herself back in that situation.

"Cheryl," Jenn answered. "From Chicago. Remember? We hooked up a few times."

Lindsey cocked her head as she mentally flipped through all the names and faces of Jenn's exes that she could remember.

"I met her at the gentlemen's club downtown when I was there for the salon and spa conference."

"Cheryl the stripper?" Lindsey announced through a mouthful of hot food.

"Shh, not so loud. And yes, Cheryl the stripper."

"Thought she became an insurance adjuster and moved to Phoenix?" She couldn't place the face, but she did remember how Jenn would beam when she talked about her.

"She did, but she flew into St. Louis yesterday to visit her aunt who isn't doing so well. She texted that she wants to see me, so she's driving down for the night."

"Wow, it's been like…"

"Ten years. Yeah, I know," Jenn said. "We reconnected on social media a couple years ago, so it'll be nice to spend the night catching up." Jenn grabbed the salt shaker and vigorously shook it over her meal. "Damn…that woman was so limber, she could actually wrap her legs around my—"

"Excuse me. I'm eating over here." Lindsey pointed to her mouthful of food and hoped Jenn would spare her the sexual details.

Jenn chuckled. "Just promise me you'll come out tonight."

"Only if you promise me you guys aren't going to play kissy face all evening," Lindsey teased.

"Deal. We'll wait until you leave," Jenn mumbled as she chewed.

Lindsey laughed. "What time and where?"

"What do you mean where? Because Jacobe is just crawling with so many gay bars?"

Lindsey playfully rolled her eyes. "What time?"

"Meet us at five for happy hour. And don't say you can't make it. A date with a novel and a glass of wine isn't an excuse for not coming out." Jenn pointed her fork at her.

"It's the perfect excuse." In fact, she couldn't think of a better way to spend the evening. The entire time she was taking care of her mom, she'd been so exhausted that she'd never had time for herself. A glass of wine and an evening reading was a luxury she couldn't afford until recently.

"Not to me it isn't. Besides, who knows, maybe tonight will be the night you meet someone." Jenn winked.

"That would imply I'm looking," Lindsey muttered.

"Says the hopeless romantic." Jenn fired back with a grin.

Lindsey shrugged. Being a hopeless romantic was one thing, finding her happily ever after was something completely different. And as wonderful as living in a small town could be, it sure wasn't helping her odds. What she needed was something, or someone, to come waltzing into her life and sweep her off her feet. Hmm, maybe Jenn was right. Maybe tonight would be the night something magical happened that would end in a date with destiny. She laughed at the thought. Yeah, like that ever happened in Jacobe, Missouri.

❖

Masquerades was a quaint bar two blocks off Main Street. A lesbian couple had bought a foreclosed home in the downturn, gutted it, and converted it into a coffee house by day, bar by night. The music was good, the food was better, and the atmosphere was easygoing. The only problem was, the same people frequented the place. Since Jacobe didn't get many out-of-towners, Lindsey pretty much knew everyone who went there. The good thing about that was she never felt awkward when she walked into Masquerades alone. There would always be a group of people she knew whom she could socialize with. On the flip side, with a bar full of familiar faces, the potential for meeting someone new was close to impossible.

"Linds, over here." Jenn shot her hand up, and Lindsey followed the beacon to a cozy corner of lounge chairs pulled around a small table. "Linds, this is Cheryl. Cheryl, Lindsey."

Lindsey extended her hand as Cheryl stood. Wow. She caught her breath. Cheryl was tall, tan, and definitely gorgeous. "Hi. Nice to meet you."

"Nice to meet you too." Cheryl gave Lindsey's hand a flirtatious squeeze.

As soon as Lindsey sat down, a cocktail server materialized by her side. "Hey, Linds, what'll it be?"

"Hey, Jessica. Could I please have a pina colada?"

Jessica placed a napkin on the table. "You got it."

Lindsey turned to Cheryl. "Jenn said you live in Phoenix, huh? Bet it's pretty hot there right now." Phoenix had never been a city that she had ever desired to visit, much less live in. As intriguing as the desert looked in pictures, it just didn't call to her. And stories of the excessive summer heat sounded miserable.

Cheryl flashed her pearly whites. "It was a hundred and fifteen when I left yesterday."

Lindsey whistled. "Shit. That's hot." Yep, definitely not her cup of tea.

Cheryl shrugged. "It can be a bitch, but you kinda get used to it. Besides, that's what swimming pools are for."

Lindsey nodded, wondering who in their right mind would live in that type of heat, with or without a swimming pool. Seriously, that was insane. "Yeah, I guess so," she mumbled back. She'd take Missouri's humidity over those temperatures any day.

As the evening progressed, Cheryl and Jenn finished off three margaritas each and were halfway through their fourth. Cheryl was now sitting in Jenn's overstuffed chair, half on her lap and half on the armrest. They were spending more time sucking each other's faces than talking. So much for Jenn's promise. Lindsey huffed as she felt more and more like a third wheel. She decided to finish up the pina colada she had been nursing and call it a night.

As Lindsey tipped her glass to swallow the last of her drink, Cheryl broke free from Jenn's lips and grabbed her strawberry margarita. "You know," she said as she raised her glass. "You guys should come to Arizona when it cools off. There're a few places in the state that are really worth seeing. Especially Sedona."

Lindsey nodded with recognition. "I read about Sedona in *L Online*. The town looks beautiful."

"Linds has a crush on the woman who writes *Gia's Gems*," Jenn said.

"I know Gia," Cheryl said. "Well, I mostly know her best friend Stacy. We kinda had a little fling a while ago. Anyway." Cheryl waved her drink in front of her face. "They both live in Phoenix too."

"Gia lives in Phoenix?" Lindsey perked up. Not that it mattered; it wasn't as though she would ever meet her. But somehow, having access to that knowledge made Lindsey feel one step closer to her.

"Yeah, Gia doesn't live that far from me. She's never around, though. From what Stacy once told me, she hasn't been out of her house in years."

"What?" Lindsey chuckled in disbelief. "How is that even possible? I follow her column. She's constantly traveling. I've seen the pictures."

Cheryl snorted. "She doesn't travel at all. Stacy let it slip one night that she is the one who travels around and takes the pictures. Then she sends them to Gia, who doctors them up and writes the articles." Cheryl finished off her drink. "Gia's like a total hermit or something like that."

"I'm having a hard time believing what you're saying." Surely, Cheryl must be referring to someone else. "I'm taking about Gia, from *Gia's Gems*."

Cheryl nodded. "Yeah, that's right. That's who I'm talking about. Stacy told me Gia's completely homebound. She never goes anywhere, not since a bad breakup did a number on her." Cheryl snickered. "According to Stacy, *Gia's Gems* is a total fake."

The pounding in Lindsey's head was deafening. Gia, a fake? Impossible. Her heart rate increased, and her breathing became slightly erratic. How could this be true? She'd lived through *Gia's Gems* in so many ways. Every month, she looked forward to reading about Gia's latest adventure. She loved her witty writing and the entertaining way she painted such vivid pictures of the people and places in each unique town. Because of Gia, she'd started a list of some of the areas she wanted to

visit someday. And now to find out she was nothing but a...
what? "A liar," she whispered through clenched teeth.

Jenn extended her leg and gently tapped Lindsey's shin.
"You okay over there, Linds? You look a little checked out."

"Hmm. What?" Lindsey got up and tossed a five-dollar
bill on the table. "I'm going to call it a night. It was nice to
meet you, Cheryl." She hoped she didn't come across short
and snappy, but damn it, Cheryl had just rocked her world and
not in a good way.

"I hope it wasn't anything I said." Cheryl presented a
dramatic pout.

Lindsey felt like screaming in all caps: *you just reached
out with your pin and popped my favorite balloon by telling
me my fantasy girl was a liar. And you're wondering if it was
something you said?*

"Linds is really into Gia." Jenn nibbled the explanation on
Cheryl's neck.

"Not anymore." The words soured on her tongue as she
headed for the door.

Lindsey bolted out of the bar, jumped in her minivan,
and sat for a moment, reflecting on the latest breaking news.
She took a few deep breaths to calm down. Wow, why such a
strong reaction over someone she didn't even know and would
probably never meet?

But she knew the answer to the question as soon as she
asked it. She was reliving unresolved feelings, as she flashed
back to her ex, Jasmine. The woman whom she'd been head
over heels in love with, and who'd betrayed her with a lie so
hurtful, it had taken years to undo.

As she headed home, she powered down the driver's
side window and leaned into the refreshing night air. Within

minutes, her anger subsided and was quickly replaced with doubt. Maybe Cheryl had it all wrong? She had seemed pretty intoxicated.

By the time she pulled into her garage, she decided to put this whole thing out of her mind. Gia was nobody to her. Why was she letting this get under her skin so much? "Because she's a liar," Lindsey answered herself. And she had an angry raw spot for people like that.

She parked between stacks of boxes—overstuffed with her mom's belongings—and stepped inside the small but quaint home that held so many memories. BeeBee, her small Yorkie mix, greeted her with a rapid display of spinning circles.

"Hi, Bee," Lindsey said her name through an exhausted breath. Why did she feel so tired? It wasn't that late, and she'd only had one drink that was mostly juice. Yet she felt completely bottomed out. As she shuffled to the couch, BeeBee darted in and out of her legs like they were poles in an agility course. "Hold on, BeeBee," she pleaded as she carefully stepped over to the coffee table. "Let me put my backpack down, then I'll pick you up." But BeeBee ramped up her attempts at getting Lindsey's attention by barking nonstop. "Oh my God, could you be any more demanding?"

BeeBee went silent for a millisecond, then let out a high-pitched whine. Lindsey tossed her backpack on the table and scooped her up. "There. Better?" She was rewarded with a face full of kisses.

She carried her into the kitchen, retrieved a small chew bone, and placed both on the floor. The bribe would keep her busy for about an hour, giving Lindsey enough time to relax and clear her mind of the evening.

She made a mug of chamomile tea and returned to her living room. A notification ding sent her digging for her phone.

She settled on the couch as she opened the text. It was from Jenn. She asked if Lindsey was okay and let her know they'd grabbed an Uber and were safely home. Lindsey replied that she was fine, just tired, and to enjoy the rest of the evening.

She tossed the phone on the coffee table, grabbed the remote, and flipped through the channels. She settled on a cold case crime show, something she was hoping would take her mind off Gia. She propped her legs up on the coffee table and tried to concentrate on the murder mystery unfolding in front of her.

But by the time she finished her second mug of tea, Cheryl's words were festering in her head. She grabbed her phone, opened Gia's webpage, and scrolled to the contact section. She fired off a diatribe on how she'd recently learned that Gia was a fake, how disappointed she was in her, and said that unless Gia came clean, she would expose her. As soon as she finished the email, her thumb hovered over the send tab for what seemed like an eternity. After all, this was the woman who'd fulfilled her fantasies. "Too bad it was all a facade." She let out a long sigh as she hit send.

She grabbed the blanket from the back of the couch, pulled it over her and stretched out. Sending the text somehow freed her anger and replaced it with a sense of contentment. BeeBee jumped up with her chew bone and nestled against her. Lindsey tried again to focus on the TV, but within minutes, her eyes became heavy, and the screen began to blur. She soon fell into a deep sleep and began dreaming about traveling to quaint little towns with Gia by her side.

CHAPTER THREE

Gia woke with a shortness of breath and what felt like the weight of the world on her chest. "Brody," she coughed out. "If you're secretly planning on suffocating me to death, you better have another servant lined up to replace me." She twisted her upper body until Brody capsized onto the bed. She maneuvered around him, grabbed her phone off the nightstand and shuffled into the kitchen for her morning routine.

She punched well-worn buttons on her coffee maker, then dumped the contents of a can of cat food on a plate. "Din-din time," she called out as she placed the dish on the floor.

She leaned against the counter, yawned a few more times, and focused on Brody. He was such a tiny thing when she'd found him shaking and scared under the bush in front of her house. When she'd reached for him, he'd melted into her hand. And now, almost five years later, he represented her most fulfilling relationship.

The beeping of the coffee pot made her turn and grab a mug. She blew across the hot liquid as she sat at the kitchen table, opened her laptop, and began checking her social feed and emails.

She played around on a variety of sites, and after she became bored, she decided to check messages from her *Gia's Gems* page. She had sixteen. Mostly people contacted her to tell her anything from how much they loved her articles to how much they loved her. Marriage proposals and offers to accompany her on her next adventure were frequent. She had a set list of prewritten replies that addressed these requests in a whimsical way that hopefully never left a fan feeling insulted or rejected. They were her readers, after all, and if not for them, she wouldn't be living her dream as a writer.

Gia cranked through her emails in no time, opening them up, one after the other as she floated to autopilot. A cute set of towels she had seen online just filled her mind when her jaw dropped. "Oh. My. God," she gasped as she leaned into the screen.

"Holy shit," she mumbled as her body started shaking, and a bead of sweat formed on her forehead. She knew sooner or later that this would happen. She was just hoping it would be later. Or better yet…never. But now someone was threatening to expose who she was. Someone who could possibly ruin all she had built with *L Online* and the other mainstream publications. Not to mention her huge fan base. "Shit, shit, shit." She grabbed her phone and fired off a 9-1-1 text to Stacy telling her to call. Seconds later, her phone jingled.

"Stacy, we've got problems," Gia spit out as she started pacing around her kitchen.

Stacy yawned in a sleepy tone. "*We* have problems, or *you* have problems?"

"*We* do. Someone figured out *Gia's Gems* is a fake, and they're threatening to expose me." Gia started rubbing the back of her neck as her stomach churned.

Stacy replied with silence.

"Did you hear what I just said?" Gia snapped in an agitated tone.

"Yes…yes I heard you." Another yawn. "Are you sure it isn't just some troll slinging shit at you?"

Gia had her share of trolls, but usually, they were homophobes blathering on about the perils of being gay. "I don't think so."

"Did this person leave a name or anything?"

Gia sat back down, focused on the screen, and squinted at the name at the bottom of the email. "Lindsey." She huffed. "It's signed Lindsey."

"Hmm, well, that definitely doesn't sound like your typical troll name."

"I know, I'm worried. What should we do?" Gia bit her nails as she bounced her leg up and down to relieve some of the anxiety surging through her. Even though she'd always known this could happen, she'd never wanted to believe it truly would. Denial was such an easier world to live in.

"Well, *you* should send her a reply and figure out what she wants. Maybe this is like a ransom note or something. You know, a pay up and I won't tell, kinda thing."

"Maybe, but she didn't mention anything about money in her email." Gia could hear Stacy mumble something inaudible. "What?"

"I was talking to…" Stacy paused for a moment. "Gail. I was telling her where the bathroom was."

Gia scoffed. "I thought you said you were going to spend the evening watching a movie and relaxing?"

"Too early in the morning for judgment, don't you think?" Stacy said in a dry tone.

Gia pinched the bridge of her nose. "Sorry, didn't mean to make that sound judgy, but I feel a major meltdown coming on over this." She wrapped her arms around her stomach as she began rocking back and forth.

"Look, reply to Linda—"

"Lindsey," Gia corrected as she began breathing her way out of a panic attack with quick short breaths.

"Lindsey, and see what she really wants. Everyone has an angle, and the fact that she contacted you before she blew the whistle means she wants something. Just reach out and... oh my..."

Gia heard soft kissing sounds as Stacy started to breathe heavy. "Focus, Stacy, focus. I need you right now."

"Mm-hmm," Stacy whispered.

"Damn it, Stacy, this isn't about your clit right now. I'm having a crisis moment."

"Mm-hmm," Stacy said as the line went dead.

Gia stared at her phone as it blinked itself back to its home screen. She huffed as she threw the phone on the table. Damn it. She jumped to her feet and began pacing again as she turned things over in her head. *Gia's Gems* was a good gig. It was finally paying off, and between *L Online* and the other publications, she had thousands of loyal readers. Not only that, but the towns she showcased always saw a bump in revenue from her column, and most reached out to her with gratitude. She was helping people, not hurting them, and she was not about to give up this gig. How dare some little Lindsey twerp threaten to expose her and everything she had built? What kind of horrible person would do that? As her anxiety morphed into anger, Stacy's words echoed in her head. Was this woman really angling for some sort of payout? What a disappointment that was going to be. Even though her writing was a fulltime gig, she didn't make *that* much money. She had enough to get by, and she had the freedom to be on her own, but that was about it. She really had nothing to offer.

Gia stared at the email as she started to calm down. Just play it cool, she told herself, and everything will be okay. She finally decided it was better not to admit to anything. That Lindsey was just fishing around, and she wasn't about to take the bait. She typed a reply that asked Lindsey why in the world she would say such a thing. "There," Gia grumbled. "Better to play offense then defense." She hit send and felt better about her morning.

By the time she was nursing her second mug of coffee, a notification came though. She took a deep breath and opened it. It was from Lindsey, and it described in detail what she'd heard from *an anonymous source.* Her stomach tightened, and she felt dizzy. Damn. The woman really did know about her secret. No mention of any money, though, just the same threat to expose her. What exactly was Lindsey's angle? *And who the hell does she think she is?*

"Okay, Lindsey," Gia said as her anger grew. "Let's see what kind of game you're playing." She fired off a four-word reply. *What do you want?* There, short and to the point. No more playing footsie.

Lindsey stared in disbelief at the exact four words she had been asking herself for years. *What do you want?* She knew Gia's question was specific to *Gia's Gems,* but she couldn't help personalizing it. Her fingers hovered over her phone's keyboard until she began asking the question of herself. *What do I want?* She thought about the dreams she'd once had, the well-thought-out plans for her life and the day all those goals and aspirations came crashing down. She frowned as she closed the screen. The four debilitating words were as much a mystery to her now as they had always been. As she was about to toss the phone on the coffee table and deal with Gia's email later, it chimed.

"Hey, Jenn." Lindsey let out a long sigh as she hit the speaker button. She felt like shit right now. What made her think it was a good idea to send Gia an email in the first place? What the hell was she thinking?

"Uh-oh, I know that tone, what happened?"

"Oh, nothing. Everything." She moaned. "I kinda did something."

"Hmm, sounds ominous. Wanna go get coffee and stuff our faces with totally unhealthy pastries at Juno's, and you can tell me all about it?"

"Where's Cheryl?" Lindsey was not in the mood for another awkward threesome this morning.

"Gone. She had to be back in St. Louis for an early morning gathering with relatives to go over some paperwork or something."

Lindsey was in a bit of a funk and wasn't really in a social mood, but what else did she have going on? Nothing. Besides, it would probably be a good idea to bounce the whole Gia thing off Jenn. She could always count on her to be brutally honest when she did something stupid. "When do you want to meet?"

"Now. I didn't get much sleep last night, which makes me too tired and lazy to make my own coffee, and you know I can't function without my fix."

Lindsey knew all too well how cranky Jenn could be when she lacked a healthy dose of caffeine. "I'll tell you what. I haven't taken Bee out for a walk yet. Why don't I swing by Juno's and pick us up some coffee and pastries and meet you at the park?"

"Deal. I'll have a large soy latte with a pump of hazelnut and a caramel pecan sticky bun. Oh, and one of their extra caffeinated coffee brownies. Did you get all that?"

"Yep, got it." Lindsey said as she shrugged her backpack on and scooped up BeeBee. "I'll meet you at the bench in thirty minutes." She hung up as Gia's four words roared back into her head. *What do you want?* "A life," Lindsey said as she settled BeeBee into the minivan and thought about her past. "I want a life."

By the time Lindsey had graduated from high school, she'd followed her friend and softball teammate, Jasmine, off to a small college in the southeast part of the state. Lindsey had majored in broadcasting, with hopes of one day working at a TV station, while Jasmine had decided to follow the field of education. By the end of their freshmen year, they had become more than friends and dormmates. They had become each other's first, and Lindsey had thought there wasn't a human alive she could love more than she'd loved Jasmine. They were inseparable, and as the semesters ticked by, they'd shared promises about a happily ever after life. Unfortunately, the summer before their senior year, Jasmine's strict upbringing had begun haunting her, and the more she'd revisited her religious roots, the more she'd become convinced that being in a gay lifestyle was wrong. She'd told Lindsey to find another dormmate and had followed it up with a text explaining why she could no longer be with her, that it was time they went their separate ways.

But Lindsey's denial was deep, and she'd held on to the hope and belief that Jasmine just needed time to figure it all out. After all, they'd made promises to each other. The day she'd stumbled upon Jasmine and a guy getting a little too cozy in a library study room, she'd lost it. When she'd confronted them, Jasmine had lied about who Lindsey was to her in a spray of sharp hateful words that had cut to the bone.

Lindsey had barely made it through her senior year. When she wasn't in class, she was in her dorm room, curled up in her bed. She'd cried so much, she'd thought the whites of her eyes would be permanently red. She'd lived on coffee and the occasional energy bar. Her grades had plummeted, and a deep depression had kicked in. She'd lost her honors standing, she'd lost weight, but most importantly, she'd lost her heart.

She would see Jasmine from time to time around campus, hanging with her boyfriend and new group of *hetero-friends*, as Lindsey had referred to them. And each sighting had pulled Lindsey into another tailspin. How could someone she'd loved so unconditionally, so wholeheartedly, turn on her so completely? But the worst betrayal came when she went home one weekend and was confronted by her family and friends. Seemed Jasmine had taken the coward's way out when explaining to everyone why she no longer wanted anything to do with Lindsey. She had spun lies of Lindsey experimenting with drugs and hanging with the *wrong kind* of people.

It had taken Lindsey months to undo all the deception. By the time graduation came, she'd wanted to get as far away as she could from Jacobe and any and all things that reminded her of Jasmine. When the offer to work for a small TV station in San Luis Obispo, California came knocking, she'd jumped at the chance. California was the place of her dreams. Both the weather and the vibe seemed so appealing, and she'd figured that, at least there, she could reinvent herself. Without giving it a second thought, she'd accepted the offer. Two weeks after graduation, she would be California bound. And she had felt it in her bones. She was going to soar out there, build a new life, and never look back.

But the week before she was to hit the road, her dad had suffered a fatal heart attack. She'd contacted the station, and with kind understanding words, they'd extended her start date by another two weeks. Lindsey had hunted for cognitive impaired facilities that could take her mom. But it soon became clear that the cost of care her mom needed was more than they could afford.

Reluctantly and with tears streaming down her face, she'd made the call to the TV station. She'd explained her current circumstances, officially declined their offer, and told them she appreciated their understanding. As the conversation came to an end, she'd closed her eyes as she'd thanked the station manager one last time, then had slowly let her finger touch the button to end the call and end all her dreams for a new life and any chance she had to get out of Jacobe.

For the next thirteen years, Lindsey had been the primary caregiver for her mom, until a few months ago, when the inevitable happened. Now that she finally had her life back, so much time had passed that she no longer recognized her dreams or aspirations. The life she'd so desperately wanted to flee from had become comfortable. Jasmine had moved out of state, and there were so many juicier rumors and scandals in Jacobe through the years that the one about her had been forgotten long ago.

As Lindsey drove to the park, she turned Gia's words over in her head. Did she want more from her life? Yes, of course she did. But she hadn't a clue how to get it or even what it looked like. What did she want? Lindsey lowered the window and let the breeze blow over her thoughts as she pondered the million-dollar question that seemed impossible to answer.

Jenn was lying on the bench, her arm folded over her face as Lindsey and BeeBee approached. "Good morning," she said as she placed the to-go cups on the ground and pulled out a mini tennis ball from her backpack. BeeBee was in motion before the ball left her hand.

Jenn groaned as she slowly sat up. "My head feels like it's going to explode."

"What did you and Cheryl do last night?"

"I'd tell you but I don't think you really want to know." Jenn rubbed her temples, then turned. "Linds, do you not like me?"

"What kind of question is that?" Lindsey stared at Jenn with concern as she scooted next to her.

"I'm your hairstylist, Linds, and I'm proud that you wear my masterpiece on your head. But every time I see you lately, you look a mess." Jenn reached out and reshaped Lindsey's hair.

"The weather has been so nice lately. It feels good having the windows down." And it helps clear my mind, Lindsey felt like adding, but refrained.

"Having the window down is one thing." Jenn continued fussing over Lindsey's hair. "Sticking your head out the window is another. You're not a dog, Linds."

"Well, thank you for that observation." She grinned as she retrieved the coffee cups and placed the bag of pastries between them. "Between the sugar and caffeine, I think we'll both be good and buzzed the rest of the day."

"As we should be." Jenn peeled the lid off her cup. "Now come to mama and slap me awake." She took several sips and closed her eyes.

Lindsey knew Jenn's ritual after a late night and left her alone while the coffee saturated her veins. She pulled her knees up to her chest, glanced across the fresh cut field and thought about all the times in her life she had been to this park. She saw herself as a toddler, squealing in delight as she ran across the field, flying a kite for the first time. She heard her scared and timid childlike voice asking her dad not to let go after he took the training wheels off her bike. And she could feel the excited anticipation as a picnic turned into a playful wrestling match that led to her first kiss with Jasmine. Lindsey released a long sigh as her heart broke a bit. That was the problem with staying in the same town she grew up in. No matter where she went, she kept bumping into her memories.

"Okay." The word came out long and slow as Jenn opened her eyes. "Now then, tell me…what happened?"

Lindsey stayed silent for a few minutes as she let the fog of the past dissipate. She watched a few dried leaves skip across an empty tennis court and heard the pastry bag rustle as Jenn dug in. *What happened?* Where to begin? She took a deep breath and felt like rephrasing that question to *what hasn't happened?* Dreams, a lover, a job. None of that had happened. So why should a fantasy about a stranger who wrote magazine articles unfold any differently? "Well." She turned to Jenn. "You know how Cheryl kinda ruined my fantasy crush with Gia last night when she told me about how she doesn't even travel to the places she writes about?"

"Sorry about that, sweetie, but knowing Cheryl, that could have been total bullshit, so take it with a grain of salt." Jenn waved in a gesture that suggested she just blow it all off.

"Well…" Lindsey stared at the ground.

"Uh-oh. What'd ya do?" Jenn took a bite out of her brownie and moaned long and loud.

Lindsey chuckled. "You do realize listening to you eat that brownie is turning me on in a weird and kinda odd way."

"Are you saying you've devolved into fantasizing about pastry porn? Because if you've become sick and twisted, then, honey, welcome to my team."

Lindsey giggled and was grateful for the momentary distraction. Jenn always had a way of lifting her spirits, and she was a godsend toward the end of her mother's life. When the stress of caregiving became more than she thought she could mentally and physically handle, she would send a text. Minutes later, Jenn would come over, sit with her mom, and play mundane games with her. This gave Lindsey a chance to get out of the house and decompress. Most of the time, she would use the break to walk around downtown. Sometimes, she would get coffee and sit for hours, staring out the window at nothing in particular as she listened to cohesive adult conversations play out in the background. Other times she would drive to the lake and sit and cry. This was not the life she'd wanted or envisioned, but it was the life she'd agreed to take on. Her parents did the best they could in providing for her. This was the least she could do to repay them.

"You were starting to say something about *Gia's Gems?*" Jenn asked.

"Right, yeah, well, I was so upset that I sent Gia an email telling her that I know she's a fake." Feeling embarrassed over her spontaneous and rather overdramatic response, she broke eye contact and picked at her pastry.

"You did not." Jenn's eyes widened.

"I did, and not only that, she replied." Lindsey frowned.

"She did not."

"She did. And guess what? She didn't totally deny it." Lindsey had hoped Gia would completely rebuff the accusation so she could be reinstated to her previous status of travel goddess. But the fact that she'd sidestepped everything and turned it back on Lindsey sank her heart and sadly confirmed the truth about what Cheryl had said.

"Shit. Cheryl was right?" Jenn leaned back.

"I guess so. I mean, Gia didn't actually come out and say she was a fake or anything like that. She just kinda ignored it." Lindsey shrugged as another wave of disappointment came over her.

"Well, did she say anything?"

"She asked me what I wanted." Linsey answered and wished she had never traveled down this road in the first place.

"And you said?" Jenn raised a brow.

"Nothing. I haven't replied." The sickening feeling resurfaced as she thought about the last exchange between them and the four haunting words that had kicked this whole big mistake right back in her lap.

"I see." Jenn finished off her brownie and chased it down with the last of her coffee. "Well, what do you want?"

Lindsey sat back and tilted her head in thought. Her eyes began welling with tears. "That's just it, I don't know. I don't know what I want or who I am anymore."

"We're no longer talking about Gia, are we?"

Lindsey shook her head and stared at her shoes as a tear escaped. Almost a decade and a half of her life was gone. Never to return. And as each year came and went, it not only marked the passing of time, it also marked the passing of opportunities. Granted, she was grateful that she was able to take care of her mom, and she'd scolded herself when she felt self-pity. Especially because—unlike her mom—she still had many more years in front of her. She could recover her life. It might not look anything like what she had once envisioned, but maybe with the right amount of patchwork, she could still soar on the wings of her dreams.

Jenn leaned in a gently nudged Lindsey's shoulder. "Hey, you have been through a lot, Linds. More than most. You gave up a career to take care of your mom, and you stayed in a town you couldn't wait to leave. The next chapter in your book of life will be all about you. But first, embrace this time of healing because when you find your footing again, you'll accomplish great things. I just know it."

Lindsey wiped her cheek with the back of her hand and nodded. She had heard the pep talk before, and she knew Jenn was right. But the heaviness that had accumulated around her heart still felt suffocating at times. "Thanks, Jenn," she choked out.

Jenn patted her thigh, then leaned back. "Are you going to respond to Gia or drop it?"

"I don't know. Probably drop it. Why, what do you think?" She was no longer feeling angry or upset with Gia. It was more like indifference. And right now, she didn't have the energy to pursue it.

Jenn paused for a long moment as she scrunched her face in thought. "I think this calls for some good old-fashioned blackmail."

"Excuse me?" Lindsey was taken aback.

"Tell her you won't expose her if she comes to Jacobe and writes an article about us. We're not a gay mecca, but for a small town, we have our share of queerness. Oh, and tell her she has to mention my salon in her article or the deal's off."

"Your salon?" Lindsey chuckled.

"Yeah, I could use the plug. Business has been slow and in a steady decline, like most of this town."

"I don't know, Jenn."

"What's not to know? Tell her that's the deal. Besides, how fun would it be to have Jacobe, the little town no one's ever heard of, in *L Online*."

Lindsey sipped her coffee in silent thought. Last night, when she'd tripped down this rabbit hole, she had been hoping it would be quickly resolved with a firm denial or that she would get no response at all. She didn't anticipate it would take this turn. And now blackmail? The palms of her hands grew clammy and she rubbed them on her shorts. As disappointing as it was that Gia appeared to be guilty by omission, Lindsey was extremely uncomfortable taking this whole thing to the level of extortion. "I'm not comfortable with this, Jenn. I don't think I can do it."

"This wouldn't be about you, Linds. It'll be about the town. Think about what it could do for Jacobe."

Lindsey released a sympathetic breath as she thought about some of the struggling shops in town, Jenn's salon definitely being one of them. "Well, I guess it would be a nice thing to do for Jacobe, even though most people around here won't have a clue what *L Online* is."

"Straight people, in general, are clueless, and for once, this isn't about them. *We* know what *L Online* is. It'll be our little spotlight of fame." Jenn smiled.

Lindsey bit into her pastry as she warmed to the thought. "If Gia agrees, are you the one who's going to show her around?"

"I have a salon to run. I won't have the time. That, my dear, will have to be on you."

"Me?" Lindsey's heart rate shot up. As if sharing the same space with the woman she had a serious crush on wasn't anxiety inducing enough. But sharing that same space after outing her as a fake and then blackmailing her? How the hell was that going to work?

"Well, yeah, I mean, someone has to show her around town, and since you're the one who kinda put this ball in motion, it makes sense that you should be the one."

"But since you're the one telling me to blackmail her into coming here, shouldn't this fall on your shoulders?"

"I told you, I have a salon to run. The only way this is going to work is if you do it." Jenn leaned over and draped her arm around Lindsey's shoulders. "Look. Just have her stay over at Paul's. That way, you'll only see her when you have to."

"She's a liar, Jenn." Lindsey folded her arms and pouted.

"Aren't we all in some way or another? Just suck it up, Linds. It'll only be for a few days. I mean, how painful could it be? She's gorgeous, witty, connected to national magazines, and you have a huge crush on her."

"Had," she grumbled.

"Okay, *had* a huge crush on her. Just remember, it's for Jacobe. Take one for the team."

Lindsey shoved her back deeper into the bench and frowned in frustration as her mind volleyed with the decision. The selfish side of her was tired of doing things for others. Even though it could provide a nice boast for the town, she just wanted to focus on herself for a while. But on the flip side, if she was being totally honest with herself—which she was trying very hard not to do—the attraction she had for Gia was still there. Meeting her *would* be a dream come true. "Oh, all right." She huffed. "I'll send out the email this afternoon with the request." She would reluctantly take one for the team.

"Don't request. Demand." Jenn punched the air. "This is blackmail, Linds, you have to demand she come here or else you'll expose her. Put on your big girl underwear. These are your terms. You're in charge."

"Right. Blackmail." The word soured on her lips. "I'm in charge. Got it."

"That's my girl. Now go out there and take no prisoners. Don't let anyone push you around ever again."

She took another sip of coffee and stared into the distance. Jenn did make some good points. Besides, if Gia was going to write about a town, why not write about her town? It wasn't like she was asking Gia to do something she wasn't already doing. Right? But blackmail or no blackmail, what was bothering her the most was the disappointment about Gia. Or was it the disappointment for herself? There was no longer anything preventing her from going after the life she'd once wanted. To make her own adventures and seek out her own gems. What was holding her back?

What do you want?

"I want to get back the one thing I gave away," she whispered. "Myself."

CHAPTER FOUR

Gia jumped every time her phone chimed. It had been hours since she'd sent Lindsey the email, and she had yet to get a reply. She was hoping the woman had a change of heart, but she doubted it. Lindsey seemed to know too many details, and if she took the time to contact Gia, she wanted something. All Gia could do now was wait. Lindsey held the cards, and that not only frightened Gia, it pissed her off. She hated feeling vulnerable, especially to someone she didn't know. It was hard to maneuver in a game where she had no idea what the rules were.

She mindlessly sat on the couch, flipping through shows she couldn't focus on. *This is ridiculous.* She headed into the kitchen. She hoped a cup of tea would help settle her stomach and soothe her nerves. As soon as she grabbed a mug, her phone dinged. She froze. Something inside her said this was the one she had been waiting for. She closed her eyes and swallowed the lump in her throat as she headed back into the main room and sank into the couch. With shaky hands, she grabbed the phone, hit the icon, and opened Lindsey's email. It was short, to the point and didn't mention any money.

Come to my hometown of Jacobe, Missouri and showcase it for your next article. Do that, and your secret will be safe with me.

Lindsey

Gia had to read the request twice to comprehend what Lindsey was asking of her. She leaned forward and buried her face in her hands as she took deep breaths. Another panic attack was surfacing, and she needed to stop it before it settled in. Ten minutes later, she leaned back and let her head rest on top of the cushion as she stared at the ceiling until the words from the email began echoing in her head. *Come to Jacobe and your secret will be safe with me.* She exhaled. "Where the hell is Jacobe, Missouri?" She reached for her phone and did a quick search. Random pictures of a typical small, midwestern town, peppered with cute little brick houses photographed in different seasons of the year, filled the page. A charming picture of downtown Jacobe decorated with holiday lights that glistened off a blanket of snow caught her attention. "That's beautiful," she mumbled as she thought about Phoenix during that time of year: still its usual brown color. She closed the pictures and fired off a text to Stacy. She let her know the blackmail request was not about money but instead about writing an article for Lindsey's hometown.

Stacy replied in seconds: *Where the fuck is Jacobe? And no, I'm not going there for you. This one's on you. It's time, Gia. Get out and see the world or in this case, a small part of it.*

The text ended with a smiley emoji that made Gia cringe, as though it was mocking her. She wanted to beg Stacy to come to her rescue, but she knew it would be futile. Stacy was right; she was on her own with this one. Her lie had finally caught up to her. She paced as she once again rubbed the back of her neck. Her brain raced through scenario after scenario of ways to get out of this, but in the end, she really had only two options: go to Jacobe or be made a fool and lose her income and fanbase.

This was not how she wanted to emerge from her comfortable cocoon. She was not ready to face the world again. And truthfully, even if she was ready, a part of her just didn't want to. Plain and simple. The little kid inside her wanted to throw one hell of a temper tantrum and tell Lindsey what she could do with herself and Jacobe, Missouri. But the adult in her took three deep breaths, surrendered, and reluctantly opened up Lindsey's email. She typed just one word: *Okay.* She knew it was time to get out of her funk. Hell, it was past time to get out of it. But damn it, she wanted to do it on her terms, not some blackmailer from Jacobe, Missouri's terms. She wanted to scream, how dare this woman, but she knew this was her own doing. Still. "How dare this woman," she yelled at the top of her lungs as she punched and kicked at the air until she was exhausted.

Seven emails later, it was decided that she would fly into St. Louis, and someone would pick her up. She would stay at Paul's Bed and Breakfast—as suggested by Lindsey—for five days and no more. In her mind, that was four and a half days more than what she would need to cover what Jacobe seemed to offer. Lindsey would be the one to show her around town. The captor watching over her conquest. Something about that just seemed twisted. "Five days." She closed her eyes and blew out a shaky breath. "You can do this. It's just five days."

The first thing she needed to do was call her mom and see if she could cat-sit Brody. Gia cradled the phone against her shoulder. "Din-din time," she called. Brody jumped on the counter and rubbed against her arms as she popped open a small can of morsels.

"Hi, sweetie," Gia's mother, Evalynn, answered in a cheery voice. "I hear my grandson."

"Yeah, I'm trying to feed him, and he's being impatient." She turned the can upside down and shook it. "In fact, he's the reason I'm calling. I was wondering if you can watch him for a few days while I, um, go on a trip."

The scream that emitted from the phone was so piercing, Gia jerked, and her phone landed facedown in the cat food, splashing a sizeable amount of gravy over her shirt and causing Brody to scatter. "Shit."

She quickly tore off several paper towels, gingerly pinched the sides of the phone, and lifted it out of the food. She wiped off the dark brown gravy as it slid down the screen protector. "Hold on, Mom. I dropped the phone in the cat food," she yelled toward the speaker. After a minute, she was content that the cleanup was as good as it was going to get. She held it up to her ear. "You still there?"

"Did you say you dropped the phone in a can of cat food?"

"Yes, because you screamed in my ear. Why did you do that? Did something happen?"

"Yes, my daughter told me she is finally getting out of the house. What or who do I owe a thank you to?"

Gia felt like saying, a despicable blackmailer, that's who. A heartless, cruel, and cold-blooded woman from Nowhere, Missouri was forcing her to take steps she wasn't ready to take. That was what she wanted to say. But instead of spending more energy explaining it all, she just said, "I think it's time."

"Henry!" Her mother's yell caused Gia to jerk again. "Gia's finally getting out of the house."

"Mom. Stop yelling."

"I told your father you're finally getting out of the house," her mom said.

"Yes, I heard you."

"He's asking me to ask you what happened."

Gia rolled her eyes. Talking to her father through her mother had become the norm, and it always irritated her. "Nothing happened. I just thought, you know, that it was time."

"What?" Her mom screamed again. Gia put the phone on speaker to prevent further hearing loss. "Your father says since you're getting out of your house now, could you come over and help him with the computer? He pressed some random button, and now a woman named Wendy keeps popping on screen showing way too much of her privates. If you know what I mean."

Gia sighed. Her dad was notorious for clicking around the computer, causing a situation or malfunction, then calling and complaining that something was wrong with the machine. "I'll call Tim and send him over." He was a local community college student who helped with any and all computer needs. She practically had him on retainer when it came to her parents.

"Thanks, honey. You know how your father can be," her mom said in a hushed tone.

"I know." Gia smiled. It was true, her dad could be a pain in the ass and very difficult most of the time. But under the gruff exterior was a soft, gentle soul. "Anyway, getting back to why I called, can you cat-sit Brody for most of next week? I can drop him off."

"You just bring that precious little muffin over here anytime."

"Thanks. I'm only planning on being gone for five days." She cringed. What the hell was she doing? For the past several years, she hadn't gone anywhere. And in less than twenty-fours, she had not only made plans to get out of her house but also made plans to get out of Arizona. She punched at the air multiple times, releasing another surge of anger as her mom continued gabbing away.

"You stay away as long as you like," her mom said. "I'm just tickled pink you're finally getting out. I always told your father that this whole isolation thing was just a temporary phase you were going through."

She snapped back to the conversation, rubbed her temples, and let out a sigh. A phase? As though all the agony she had felt over the breakup that put this whole ball in motion was just a phase? She took another breath as the need to defend herself surfaced. *Don't go there.* She calmed down and reminded herself that anything she did that her mom disapproved of was always dismissed as *just a phase.* Hell, under that definition, Gia's entire life could be summed up as one big disappointing phase. She pinched the bridge of her nose and tried to sound upbeat. "Thanks, Mom, I'll bring him over Sunday night and pick him up that following Saturday."

"That's fine, dear. Now I need to go. Your father is pointing the wrong end of the remote at the TV, and it's getting the best of his temper."

"Go rescue dad. I'll see you guys Sunday."

"Henry, how many times have I got to tell you…" The line went dead, and Gia shook her head. As much as she loved and adored her parents, they were exhausting. They were oil and water and the fact that they were still together amazed her. She didn't know if that was a testament to their stubbornness or represented a special—but seemingly dysfunctional—kind of love. "Maybe it's a generation thing," she muttered as she grabbed her phone and headed into the main room. She thought about her ex and questioned if there really was such a thing as a functional relationship. She burrowed into the couch, let out an exhausted sigh, and let the haunting memories she blamed for the mess she found herself in dance in her head.

Gia had met Audrey after a friend had set them up on a dinner date. They'd hit it off, and two months later Audrey had moved in with her. But Audrey had abusive demons that reared their head when things didn't go her way. Gia saw hints of them early on, but damn, the sex was good, and Audrey's talks of change were smooth. By their fifth year, the cracks in the relationship were almost too many to repair, but Gia still held hope that they could work it out. Two weeks before their first couples' therapy appointment, Audrey had announced she was in love with another woman. By the end of that week, she had moved out. And as much as Gia didn't want to admit it, a part of her heart went with her.

Gia had turned her hurt inward, shutting people and the world out. And before she knew it, she was looking in the rearview mirror so much, she wasn't paying attention to her life zooming by in front of her. That view was impossible to see through the lingering haze of pain and anger. Her therapist once told her to compare her healing process to headlights in dense fog. "Even though it's hard to see the road in front of you," her therapist had told her. "Just concentrate on what you can see, and bit by bit, you'll make it to your destination." But Gia still felt like she was miles away from where she needed to be.

CHAPTER FIVE

Hey, Jenn." Lindsey said the name as one big yawn. She had been up most of the night, contemplating her financial future with concern. Soon enough, she would have to start sending out a resume. But the only thing she had experience in was caregiving. And as much as she admired those that chose it as a profession, she needed to find something that for her, wasn't as emotionally draining.

"Someone's a sleepyhead this morning. Late night, I take it?"

"Yeah, I couldn't sleep, so I ended up crunching the numbers again to see how much I really can afford to spend on all the needed repairs, which depressed me. And then…oh, I don't know. I guess I kinda just drifted over to—"

"You got on Jasmine's page again, didn't you?" Jenn interrupted.

Lindsey grumbled. Every time she felt sorry for herself, she pulled up Jasmine's social media page. She knew it was a dysfunctional and toxic thing to do, but she didn't care. She was looking for evidence that her ex-lover's life was in some form of shambles. Not that she wished bad things for her, but if ever the universe decided to serve Jasmine her own medicine, that would be fine with Lindsey. "Yeah. I got on Jasmine's page again, and she still seems happily married to Brad the Ogre," she said with all the disgust she could muster.

"Linds..."

"I know. You don't have to say it." Even though the pain from the breakup was long gone, the bitterness still lingered. Jasmine had what seemed like a happy and fulfilling marriage with someone, while Lindsey had nothing. No amazing relationship or beautiful vacation pictures to post. After giving up a chunk of her life, she had nothing to show for it. But in her heart, she knew that wasn't totally true. She had been given the gift of time with her mom. Something she would have never had if she was in California. And in the end, when her mother was completely bedridden, Lindsey still made sure she had her dignity. All the things that mattered the most in life weren't always measured in pictures and wealth. She needed to remind herself of that more often.

"Okay. Then change of subject. What time you going to the airport to pick up Gia?"

Lindsey tapped her phone and glanced at the clock. "Her flight gets in at three."

"Good, between now and then, can you do me a favor?"

"What's up?"

"Paul's out of shampoo and gel, and I'm swamped at the salon. Can you swing by and pick up some product to bring to him before you head up to St. Louis? He said he has enough to last another day or two, but you know how he can be about his hair."

"Yes, I do. I'll be by in an hour."

"Thanks. Now tell me, what are you wearing?" Jenn asked.

"Now?" Lindsey glanced at her faded blue jeans and white V-neck T-shirt.

"Not now. When you go to pick up Gia."

"The same thing I have on now, which just happens to be the same thing I always wear. Why?" Jenn had been hounding her for months to up her fashion game so she could "snag a babe and get laid."

"First impressions are lasting impressions," Jenn said.

"I don't want to make a lasting impression. I just want her to write a good article about the town." Lindsey grumbled.

"Linds, you've been crushing on this woman for years."

"Those days are gone." Sort of. The anxiety churning in her stomach over picking Gia up was testament that the disappointment hadn't completely overshadowed the crush.

"Uh-huh, well, at least take this piece of advice, don't drive with your window down."

"But it's a beautiful day," Lindsey whined.

"Yeah, I know, honey, but trust me on this one, okay?"

Lindsey laughed. "Okay, I'll keep it under advisement."

"That's my girl. See you in a bit."

Lindsey ended the call, glanced at her clothes, and wondered if she should change. Unfortunately, the blackmail had already made the first impression, and it wasn't a good one. She could probably dress in the sexiest of outfits and still not reverse that train. Too bad because a part of her really wanted to believe they might have actually hit it off. Oh well, just one more missed opportunity to add to her list.

Gia fastened her seat belt on the plane and took a deep breath as she tried to calm her nerves. She had been online with her therapist every day crying, pouting, and feeling sorry for herself. Her therapist, like Stacy, had tried to put a positive spin on the situation. But Gia had refused to listen to either of them. All she could focus on was the negative. She closed her eyes and placed her index finger to her thumb and took a deep breath. Last night, her therapist had walked her through the meditative steps of positive mindfulness. She tried to clear her head and channel her therapist's voice telling her to relax and be in the moment. But as soon as the plane pushed back from the gate, her leg began to bounce so much, she abandoned her meditation attempt and stared out the small window.

She yawned as she focused on the other planes parked at their gates. She didn't get much sleep last night, and by four in the morning, she gave up and got up. She yawned again. What was she doing? She rubbed the sweat off her hands and onto her jeans. She cursed Audrey for making her such a freak, and she cursed Lindsey for making her shed her protective shield.

Gia's phone dinged a notification from Stacy: *You on the plane?*

Yes, about to take off, Gia replied.

I'm so excited for you!

Gia frowned. *I've been on planes before.*

Not in over 5 years.

I haven't had sex in that same amount of time. Will you cheer me on when I break that streak too?

You've had sex since then, just not with someone else. Insert vibrator emoji.

Gia laughed. She might have shut herself off from the outside world, but her inner self still wanted to go for a ride from time to time. The flight attendant began her list of announcements as the plane taxied to the runway. *Gotta close it down. I'll text when I land.*

A heart emoji appeared as she powered down her phone. She tossed it in her purse, leaned back, and closed her eyes. She wished she was home with Brody, relaxing in her comfort zone and letting the world go by. She actually enjoyed her isolated way of life, embraced it, even. And why not? It was easy. No people drama, no hassles dealing with ever-increasing city traffic, and no obligations. She had built a world that satisfied almost all her needs, and now she was being forced out in the open, pulled out of her hibernation before she was ready to face the world. She would fulfill the blackmail request because she had no choice. But as soon as she was done, she wanted to return to her predictable life in her self-made bubble.

"Five days." She sighed and folded her arms tightly across her chest as the plane accelerated down the runway, ascended, and banked east. Just five days. *You can do this.*

Lindsey stood on the other side of the security check-in holding a small cardboard sign with *Gia* scribbled in block letters. She scanned the sea of people walking toward her. A shiver tickled up her spine. She was going to finally meet Gia. Granted, not under the best circumstances. But who knew, maybe if they got to know each other, Gia could forgive the blackmail.

Ah yes. Lindsey crinkled her nose. The blackmail. That little disappointing reminder that the reason Gia was here in the first place was because she was a liar. And there was no way Lindsey was going to go down that road with someone like that again. She chuckled at herself, as if those feelings were a two-way street. She just had to get through the next five days, then they'd both get back to whatever it was that resembled their lives.

❖

Gia saw her name on the pink cardboard sign as soon as she rounded the corner. The woman holding it was adorable. Her breath caught at the unexpected shiver. *Is that her? Could that possibly be the little blackmailer?* She raked her eyes over the athletic woman sporting faded jeans, a tight white T-shirt and short windblown hair. Since the email just said *someone* would pick her up, she hoped *this* someone, who was starting to stir something deep inside her, was not Lindsey. *Please, please, please let this woman not be her.*

"I'm Gia." She shuffled up and stared into the most beautiful, crystal blue eyes she had ever seen. It was as if the universe was rewarding her for making this intolerable journey.

The woman extended her hand. "I'm Lindsey."

Great. Just great. Gia's smile faded as she half-heartedly shook Lindsey's hand. On second thought, the universe must really hate her.

"Do you have luggage?" Lindsey asked.

"One bag," Gia grumbled as her little burst of enthusiasm morphed into annoyance.

"Baggage claim is this way." She cocked her head.

"So the sign says." Gia snapped, then scolded herself for sounding like a bitch, something she'd never regarded herself as being. But she was tired, stressed, and feeling vulnerable. She was not here under her own free will. And even though her captor was cute and stirred some interesting feelings, she was here under duress. Everything about this was just wrong. She hiked her purse higher on her shoulder as she followed Lindsey, who hopefully hadn't heard her comment. And if Lindsey did, oh well. Under these circumstances, she had a right to be a little bitchy.

They rode the escalator in silence. Day one of captivity had begun, and Gia felt like she was barely holding on. The irritability that had been building all week was on the verge of exploding into a full-blown meltdown, and she needed some alone time to get a better handle on herself. "I'm going to use the restroom. I'll meet you at the carousel."

"What was your flight number?" Lindsey asked.

"Two thirty-nine."

"That's carousel number three." Lindsey pointed.

Gia nodded as she veered off. She quickly locked herself in a stall and sat. She put her head between her knees as she took deep breaths. The noise of the airport, the crowds moving around her, and her unexpected attraction for Lindsey was crashing in on her. Tears of frustration dripped from her eyes. Being a hermit for the past several years had turned her into someone she no longer recognized. She used to enjoy being out and about and had always looked forward to vacations. *What have I become?*

She hugged herself and gently rocked. "I'm pathetic," she whispered. She took a few more deep breaths, unrolled a wad of toilet paper, and dabbed her face. Like it or not, she was here, and for the next few days, she had to act like a functioning adult. She had stayed far too long at her one-person pity party, and for the first time in years, she felt the sensation of being lonely. "You can do this," she said as she stood, took another deep breath, and unlocked the stall. She checked herself in the mirror and tried to see the person that she'd once been. She gave herself a reassuring nod and headed to carousel number three.

Gia pulled her phone out to text Stacy that she'd landed and that she would call when she'd settled in. Not wanting to engage with Lindsey, she mindlessly stared at emails and websites. They might have an agreement, but that didn't include an obligation to be friendly or social. At least not for now. She was still on sensory overload, and she really needed to cocoon herself off from the world. If not physically, then mentally.

Twenty minutes later, the buzzer sounded, and the blue light flashed as the carousel fired up. Gia's luggage was the fifth one up the ramp, and as soon as it dropped, she announced, "That black one's mine. The hard shell with the purple luggage tag." She raised a brow as she slightly cocked her head. Since Lindsey had dragged her halfway across the country, she could damn well fight through the crowd to get her bag.

Lindsey nudged her way up and grabbed Gia's suitcase as it swung around. She heaved it off the carousel, hiked up the handle, and wheeled it over.

"Thanks." Gia reached for it. "I can handle it from here."

"I got it," Lindsey said as she nodded toward the sliding doors. "I'm parked out this way."

"Okay." Gia shrugged as she dropped her phone back in her purse and followed her into the overcast skies and thick humid air. By the time they'd walked to Lindsey's minivan, she was dripping with sweat. She tugged at her shirt in an attempt to unstick it as Lindsey unlocked the car. Gia hopped in and fanned her shirt.

"Yeah," Lindsey said as she flung Gia's suitcase in the back and settled into her seat. "The humidity can really be a bit stifling."

The words, *ya think*, were on the tip of Gia's tongue, but instead she just nodded as she fastened herself in. And people complained about Phoenix's heat, she thought as she wiped the back of her hand over her forehead. She glanced out the window and silently cursed Lindsey for dragging her to this dreary, sweltering place. Why couldn't she be from Hawaii or Cancun? Gia closed her eyes and pressed her forehead against the window. Hopefully, Lindsey wasn't in the mood for conversation because right now, she had nothing good to say. She just wanted to get through the next few days with minimum human contact and get back to her life. Five days of torture and she would be free.

Gia opened her eyes and glanced at Lindsey. She had her window down, and the breeze tousled her hair. Gia's nipples hardened as a tingle tickled its way up her spine. *God, she really is adorable.* She mentally hand slapped her face and cursed her body's reaction as she once again focused out the window. She was not about to have any feelings for this… this…this unpleasant but sexy-as-hell woman. Gia sighed as her nipples ignored her by remaining excited and erect. This was going to be a long week.

The sun was setting as Lindsey pulled off the highway and onto side roads lined with corn and soybean fields. Gia cynically thought the place should have been named Podunk instead of Jacobe. But as they passed quaint little brick homes with well-manicured lawns and cute wraparound porches, she softened her opinion. Not only were the homes charming, but everything was just…

"So green. Everything is so green," she said in a low voice as she powered down her window.

"Yes, it is. And I know this probably doesn't look like much, especially coming from a huge city and all, but here we are. What it lacks in size, it makes up for in charm."

"So this is…"

"Main Street, yes. Welcome to downtown Jacobe."

Gia nodded as she looked at the buildings. Nothing was over two stories tall, and chain restaurants and retail stores seemed to be in the minority, which she found refreshing. She tried to visualize the street under a blanket of snow, with holiday lights strung from building to building like in the pictures. Downtown Jacobe definitely had character and charm, she reluctantly admitted to herself.

At the first stoplight, Lindsey took a left, and two blocks later, stopped in front of a two-story, dark red brick house with off-white trim and a wraparound porch. The front yard was impeccably manicured. Flowers were in full bloom in a variety of colors, and a wooden sign read *Paul's Bed and Breakfast*.

"Here we are. Paul's Bed and Breakfast."

Gia almost shot back, *so the sign says*, but caught herself. One bitchy comment was enough for one day. She slowly got out and stretched as Lindsey retrieved her luggage.

A thin short man in his mid-thirties came bounding out of the front door and into Lindsey's open arms. He gave her a peck on each cheek, then turned and extended his hand to Gia. "Name's Paul. Welcome."

"Thank you," Gia softly said as she shook his hand. "Um, your place is nice."

"Just you wait until you see the inside. Jeff and I spent all winter redecorating, didn't we, Linds?"

"Yep, and you guys did a great job."

Gia pulled the handle up on her luggage and started to wheel it down the brick walkway.

"Where are my manners?" Paul shooed her away. "I've got this." He tried to pick up the suitcase but slammed it back down. "Holy shit, what do you have in here?"

"I uh, didn't know what to expect, so I may have overpacked." She smiled, feeling a hint of embarrassment.

"That's okay." Paul wheeled the luggage behind them. "It's always nice to have options."

"I can get that, really, it's not a big deal."

Paul waved her off. "You're my guest, and this is one of our services."

Gia looked over Paul's thin frame and five-foot-four height. She calculated that she could probably bench press more than he weighed. As sweet as his chivalry was, there were cases where it seemed a bit ridiculous, this being one of them.

He opened the screen door and let Gia step into the house. She was greeted by a beautiful great room decorated in forest green and offset with the same off-white as the outside trim. The colors complemented each other well and gave the interior a cozy, yet elegant feel. "Your room is upstairs, the first door on the right."

He pushed past her, and she cringed as he pulled on her suitcase, clunking it loudly into each wooden stair they climbed. "Normally, Jeff handles the luggage." Paul huffed. "But he's visiting his parents in Oklahoma right now, so I'm holding down the entire fort."

"Besides being Paul's husband, Jeff is the town's semi-famous resident," Lindsey said from behind Gia. "He's a body builder, and he's won three—"

"Four," Paul interrupted.

"Four reginal competitions," Lindsey said.

"We fit perfectly together." Paul grunted. "He exercises his muscles, and I exercise my cooking skills. We're each other's other half."

He took a couple of heavy breaths, arched his back, and wheeled the case into the bedroom. Gia stepped around him to take in a room that had a queen-size canopy bed with dark walnut furniture. The room itself flipped the colors, and the walls were tan with green trim. Fresh cut flowers filled the vase on the nightstand, and she nodded her approval. "It's beautiful."

"Thank you." He settled her luggage by the dresser. "I made a roast for dinner. If you'd like, I can heat some up for you?"

"Oh...uh," Lindsey stuttered. "I was going to take her over to Marcello's."

Paul crinkled his face. "Why?"

"Because I knew you would have already made dinner, and Marcello's serves until nine."

"Actually," Gia groaned. "I'm not feeling that hungry, so I think I'll skip dinner tonight and just settle in."

"Why don't I heat up a little something and bring it up? If you eat it, fine, if not, no big deal. I kind of know my way around a kitchen pretty good."

Gia wanted to shout that the only thing she wanted was to go home and not be here. She was exhausted, the humidity was suffocating, and socializing with people, especially strangers, hadn't been her thing in years. Hibernating was her thing. It was what she did best. But instead, she took a deep breath and nodded. "Thank you. Now, if you don't mind, I think I'll take a shower and relax." She turned, effortlessly hoisted her luggage onto the foot of the bed, and began unzipping the sides.

"Well, I, uh, guess I'll see you in the morning," Lindsey said.

"Mm-hmm," Gia mumbled without looking up. She figured seeing the town would take all of, what, a half hour, at most?

"Good night then." Lindsey mumbled as Gia heard them leave.

She promptly shuffled over to the door, closed, and locked it. She put her back against the wall and slowly slid down until she sat on the floor. She bent her legs to her chest and tightly folded her arms around them. Her head was pounding, and she could feel another anxiety attack coming on. She needed to pull herself together, or she would never get through the next few days. "Gia," she whispered to herself, "when did your life take such a fucked-up turn?" And how was she ever going to get it back?

❖

Paul walked Lindsey out to her car and leaned through her open driver's side window. "She's much cuter in person. A little stiff around the edges but definitely a looker," he said.

"You think so?" What a disappointment Gia was turning out to be. Lindsey sighed as she buckled herself in. Maybe this whole thing had been a mistake. Maybe she should have just let the whole thing go. But the business owners of the town would appreciate the plug. When else would little Jacobe, Missouri be featured in any national magazine? *Never*. She was doing the right thing.

Paul threw his head back in laughter. "Oh please, Linds. You may be in a dry spell, but I know your parts still work."

"That's such a guy thing to say."

"I learned all my smut talk from Jenn, so there." He stepped away from the car. "I'm just saying is all."

"Oh, speaking of Jenn, I almost forgot." Lindsey leaned over the passenger seat and handed him the hair products. "She said to give you this."

He opened the bag. "Tell her thank you, and when Jeff gets back, we'll all have to go out."

"I'll let her know." Lindsey waved as she pulled away. Paul was right; of course he was. She was physically attracted to Gia, that was a given, and she had fantasized about her for years. But besides the physical, Gia was definitely not what she wanted.

What do you want? Those four haunting words came screeching back into Lindsey's head. "Well," she mumbled to herself. "I don't want a woman who's a liar and one who's so off center. And so uptight, withdrawn, bitchy, and unapproachable," she said in a singsong kind of way. But one thing was for sure, her body definitely responded as she thought about Gia's beauty. She looked down as her crotch throbbed. "Oh, get a grip."

As she headed for her house, she leaned into the evening air. Despite Gia's frigid personality, she definitely checked off a lot of boxes for Lindsey. *Oh well. Guess you can't have everything.* She exhaled a long sigh. It was sadly becoming the story of her life.

❖

Gia tipped her luggage on its side and let the contents pour onto the bed. She rifled through her clothes until she found a pair of blue cotton boxers and an old T-shirt. How the hell did everyone handle the humidity? At least Phoenix was a dry heat. She laughed at herself for repeating the cliché she'd heard so many locals say when they defended living there. She stripped out of her sweaty clothes, leaving them in a pile on the bathroom floor as she stepped into the shower. She stayed in there for over twenty minutes as she let the water rinse away the day. By the time she finally stepped out and wrapped herself in a plush ivory towel, all she wanted to do was fall into bed and sleep. A knock on the door startled her.

"Yes?"

"I left a tray of food outside your door." Paul's muffled voice was barely audible.

"Thanks," Gia called back. She tugged a pair of clean clothes on, pulled the tray in, then quickly relocked the door. Privacy was what she needed right now. A big dose of *leave me the fuck alone.* She had no intention of eating, but as the smell began permeating the room, her stomach growled. Ten minutes later, she was licking the empty plate, moaning and feeling much better. Damn, he wasn't kidding when he said he knew his way around a kitchen. That was one of the best meals she'd had in a long time.

Gia's phone jingled. "Hey, Stace."

"Well, you answered, so that's a good sign. How's it going with the blackmailer?"

Gia paused for a moment as the adorable smiling face with the messy hair popped into her head. "She's okay, I guess."

"Wait a minute. The woman you've cussed out hourly since this whole thing started and consistently called the wretched blackmailer is now okay?"

"What do you want me to say, Stace?"

"Ouch, someone's cranky."

Gia closed her eyes, pinched the bridge of her nose and made a note that she needed to address her newfound bitchiness in her next therapy session. "Sorry, that was uncalled for. I'm just tired and way out of my comfort zone."

"Apology accepted. Now, wanna answer my question in more detail because I'm just dying to know."

"She's, um, well she's…kinda cute, actually, and the bed and breakfast I'm staying at is run by this guy who made me the most delicious dinner I think I've ever eaten." She caught herself smiling, then quickly frowned. What was she doing? She rested her forehead in her hand. In the days leading up to this, she had worked herself into a hatred toward Lindsey and the little town she was forced to come write about. Now, with a full belly and warm, lavender scented skin, she was almost feeling herself again.

"Well, well, sounds promising. Send pics"

Gia snorted at the irony. "I will. How's it going on your end?"

"Great, I have a date tonight with the bartender I told you about."

"The one you met last night?"

"The same. And after I finish up tomorrow, I'll have a week off to relax around the house and…hey, why don't I change my flight and come to St. Louis? I can rent a car and drive to Jackson."

"Jacobe," Gia corrected.

"Right, Jacobe, and hang with you for a while. Then we can fly back together."

"Really?" Gia squealed. Trying to be a functioning adult would be so much easier with Stacy by her side.

"Well, yeah. Unless of course, you'd rather I—"

"Oh my God, Stace, I'd love you forever if you came out here." Gia's spirits soared. Stacy could command the attention of any room. Having her here would allow Gia to hide in her shadow.

"Well, unfortunately, I can't be there for another day, but hey, that's better than nothing, right?"

Disappointment crept into Gia's hope. "Yeah. I guess. You sure you can't come sooner?" The thought of spending all day tomorrow with Lindsey terrified her. Lindsey both infuriated and intrigued her.

"You've got this, Gia."

Gia spread out on the bed and let her head rest on the pillow. Both were surprisingly comfortable. "I don't know, but I'm feeling another panic attack coming on."

"Just breathe, it's only a few days, not a lifetime. You said Lindsey was cute, so enjoy spending some time with her."

"She's a blackmailer," Gia grumbled.

"And you're a liar. The two of you make the perfect crime duo. Oops, gotta go, my date awaits."

"Have—" But before she was able to finish her sentence, the line went dead. "Fun," Gia said as she let the phone drop onto the bed. She let out a long breath and draped her arm across her eyes. *Just get through tomorrow, and then Stace can run interference for you.* "You've got this." She smiled with a renewed sense of hope. "You've got this."

❖

"Hey, Jenn." Lindsey and BeeBee strolled into her salon.

"Lock the door behind you," Jenn said as she swept up a pile of hair. "I should have closed down hours ago, but Mrs. Jensen insisted she had to have a cut and color for her niece's birthday party tomorrow."

"Thought her niece was only two."

"Yep. And don't try to reason it away. I already have, and I came up with nothing." Jenn knocked the contents of the dustpan into the trash. "Why don't you grab a couple of drinks out of the back fridge. There's also a new bag of chews for Bee in the cabinet. I should be done here in a sec."

Lindsey brought back two beers, placed them on the counter, and sank into a salon chair as BeeBee jumped on her lap. She handed Bee the petite chew bone and smiled at a distant memory of BeeBee contently lying in her mom's lap, chewing on a bone and listening to an endless sea of stories stuck on repeat. BeeBee and her mom had shared a special bond. And long after her mother's eyes lacked any recognition for Lindsey, she still could identify little Bee. On the last day of her mom's life, when the hospice nurse had announced she was slipping away, Lindsey had placed BeeBee by her side and gently guided her mom's hand down Bee's back. Her mother's lips had turned up for the first time in months as she'd pushed out her last words, "BeeBee."

"Phew," Jenn said as she grabbed a beer and settled into the chair next to Lindsey. She wiped a thin layer of sweat from her forehead as she opened her bottle. "Well." Jenn grinned. "I'm dying to hear how things went with Gia."

"She's, um, she's cuter in person than in her picture." Lindsey smiled as she felt a flash of heat tickle its way across her face.

Jenn leaned over and smiled. "Really? And is that a gleam of lust I see sparkling in your eyes?"

"What? No, Gia's still an awful person, she's just..." Lindsey flashed back to the moment she'd seen Gia at the airport. "A beautiful awful person."

"Oh, I see." Jenn settled back into her chair. "She's back to being Gia? Ever since this started, you've only referred to her with phrases like, the loathsome liar."

"That hasn't changed. She's still a liar." Lindsey paused for a moment and took a sip of beer. "We sat in silence almost the entire ride from the airport."

Jenn raised a brow.

"I'm not kidding. We barely spoke," Lindsey looked down as she scratched BeeBee's head.

"Well, that sounds painful."

"It was." Lindsey frowned. Part of her had hoped the two-hour ride to Jacobe might give them a chance to get to know each other. Maybe she could even talk about why Gia faked her column. *But I guess forcing her to come here didn't set the best tone between them.* Expecting anything more than what they'd agreed on was setting herself up for more disappointment. She should be content that Gia was here. Friendship and conversation were never a part of the deal. It was only a part of Lindsey's hopefulness, and that was a far cry from reality.

"Where're you going to take her tomorrow?" Jenn guzzled half the bottle.

"I thought I'd take her to the river. For a float trip." It would not only showcase a beautiful part of the area, but she had hoped it would also provide them with some one-on-one time to get to know each other a little better.

"A float trip? On her first full day?"

"Well, yeah. I was thinking we could float for a while, then have lunch at The Non-Float Float Stop. Then head back. Why? Do you think that's a bad idea?" It had been a while since Lindsey had been inner tubing, and she'd chosen the activity as a throwback to the enjoyment the river provided every summer when she was a kid. She thought it would be nice to share the memory and a little piece of herself with Gia. But doubt set in as she looked at Jenn's face.

"I mean, don't get me wrong," Jenn waved her beer. "That sounds like a fun day to me and you, but for a city girl from the desert?"

"I think she'll love it." Or was that statement more about herself than Gia? That river held so many wonderful memories of her childhood. Happier times when her life was so much lighter, responsibilities were almost nonexistent, and love was still an obtainable fairy tale. She was hoping a day on the river would not only bring her closer to Gia but also closer to a time in her life when she'd still believed the wings of her dreams would carry her away. Before time caught up to her and life began to beat her down.

CHAPTER SIX

I already hate today." Gia's phone was on speaker as she searched through her suitcase for a pair of board shorts and a matching sports bra. She was feeling much better than she had in the past week. A stomach full of delicious food, a comfortable bed, and the background sound of nature instead of cars had created a restful night's sleep. And she woke to the wafting smell of cinnamon baking in the kitchen. Although still a bit on edge, her crankiness had dialed down several notches, and her bitchiness about her predicament didn't feel as consuming. Maybe it was because Stacy was coming in tomorrow, and she would have a familiar safety blanket to wrap herself up in. Or maybe it was because there was a glimmer of the old Gia peeking though. Whatever the reason, the outcome was causing her to feel a bit more centered.

"You're really floating down a river?" Stacy asked.

"Apparently." Gia grumbled as she scrutinized her clothes. When she'd packed the other night, she was so pissed off, she'd thrown a bunch of random clothes in because she didn't care. Now, as she was going through them, nothing seemed to feel quite right. And caring about how she looked suddenly seemed to matter.

"As in, the Mississippi river?" Stacy's voice went up an octave.

"No, more like a little river creek thing. I think."

"Definitely not my choice for a first date, but whatever."

"It's not a date, Stace. It's blackmail, remember? She's forcing me to do this. It's part of her demands. I should be at home right now, cleaning up Brody's vomit, resting comfortably on my couch, and not dealing with people in any capacity. You know, my normal life. Not putting my ass in an innertube that was designed for a car and floating down some waterway. I think Lindsey planned this as some form of punishment."

"Just be careful. You know what always happens in those creepy backwoods' horror movies. Some scary ass guy comes out of nowhere, chases you down, and either kills you or kidnaps you."

Gia stood in stunned silence. "I can't believe you said that. Now how am I supposed to get that out of my head after you planted it there?" She wiggled into her shorts and sports bra.

"What? It happens all the time, and you know it. Just keep an eye out is all I'm saying."

"Do I have a choice?" Gia checked herself in the mirror and nodded.

"No. I'm sure everything will be fine, and you'll have a wonderful day."

"You know, you could have led with that instead of the psycho backwoods murdering kidnapping thing?" She gathered the pile of clothes and shoved them back into an empty dresser drawer.

"Now, what fun would that be? Don't forget to take pictures. You're supposed to be writing an article. Love you. Bye."

Gia grabbed the plastic cover for her phone and shoved her driver's license and two twenties in the pouch. When Lindsey had told her to bring a waterproof case, along with a swim outfit, she'd figured they would be poolside, not on some river doing God knew what. She also, per Lindsey's instructions, shoved a change of clothes in a beach tote. She checked herself one last time and let out a breath. Day two was about to begin, and although she felt much more confident and put together, there was still lingering resentment for being here. She'd already calculated that if they floated for a couple of hours, she could call today good enough. She would make excuses to kill the rest of the day in her room, and that would make two days officially in the books. Stacy would come to her rescue tomorrow, and with that in mind, this whole blackmail thing seemed less scary and somewhat doable. "You've got this." She nodded to herself in the mirror.

As she headed downstairs, the wonderful smell of cinnamon overwhelmed her. She smiled. "Damn," she said softly as she walked into the kitchen. "That smells amazing."

Paul was leaning into an open oven. He pulled out two trays of cinnamon rolls and set them on cooling racks. "Jeff always tells me the smell of my sticky buns could wake the dead. I take that as a compliment." He separated one and placed it on a small plate. He spread a thick layer of icing on top and finished it off with a sprinkle of chopped nuts. He slid the plate over to Gia, leaned against the counter, and watched her.

She had never been one for sweets, but the smell was so enticing, she couldn't help but graciously accept. After the first bite melted in her mouth, she moaned and knew she would finish every last morsal.

"I'll take that as a compliment too. Where you off to today?" He pushed off the counter and started icing the rest of the batch.

"River rafting. Then lunch at some no-floating place," she mumbled as she chewed.

"The Non-Float Float Stop. They're food's not bad, considering they only have a few sandwiches to choose from. Order the veggie deluxe. It's the best thing on their menu."

"I will." Gia licked her fingers as she regarded him. "Paul. Can I ask you something?"

"You can ask me anything." He smiled.

"This river. Is it um, you know?" Gia lowered her voice as she leaned in a bit.

His brows shot up. "Know what?" he whispered. "Is this a trick question? Because I love word play."

"Is the river at all creepy in a horror movie, backwoods' murder kidnapping kind of way?"

He leaned back and laughed. "You've been watching way too much TV. Let me put it to you this way. I…" He rubbed his hand down his body for reference. "Go floating on that river all the time. If there was even a hint of creepy out there, do you honestly think I would be anywhere near that place?"

"I think I get the picture." Gia smiled with relief as she heard a horn honk. "Oh, I think that's my ride. Thank you again for breakfast. It was delicious."

"Yet again, my buns have lived up to their reputation, and you can take that any way you want. Now go have a fun day. But before you go." He grabbed two rolls, sprinkled chopped nuts, and strategically placed them in a plastic container. "These are for you and Linds."

"Thanks, Paul." Gia took the container and walked out the front door. She approached Lindsey's minivan and handed her the sticky buns as she buckled up. She glanced at Lindsey and reluctantly let a butterfly take a lap around her stomach. As much as it pained her to admit it, she couldn't deny the attraction.

Lindsey popped open the container and took a whiff. "Oh man, Paul makes the best sticky buns."

"I know. I just had one, so go ahead and eat both if you want."

Lindsey grabbed a roll and took a big bite. "You, um, you ready for this?" she mumbled as she glanced at Gia.

"No, but do I have a choice?" Gia placed her tote on the floor behind her seat. She noticed two black innertubes and a stack of neatly folded beach towels. She swallowed the lump building in her throat. Was she really going to stick her ass in that tube and float down a river? She had never done that before because she had never found it appealing. Boating on lakes was appealing, and floating on a raft in a pool was pleasantly enjoyable. But this? She closed her eyes and took another meditative breath. Just get through the day. *You've got this.*

"Nope." Lindsey threw the car in drive and headed for the highway.

The road trip was another repeat of yesterday's silent ride. Thirty minutes later, they were driving across a one-lane bridge. Gia craned her neck as a group of five inner-tubers lazily floated under the bridge. The sun glistened off the clear water, and the surrounding lush green foliage made her smile. She had forgotten how truly beautiful this type of scenery was. Not that the desert wasn't beautiful; it was so sparse and barren compared to this. *This really would make the perfect backdrop for a murder.* Goddammit, she grumbled to herself.

She knew Stacy's comments would somehow work their way into her brain. She shook her head to clear the thought as Lindsey pulled down a small dirt road that ended in a clearing at the river's edge.

Gia slowly opened her door and stepped onto the rocky riverbank. She was greeted with the loud sounds of frogs croaking and insects buzzing. The frogs she could handle, but the flying insects that were making it their mission to invade her personal space were another story.

"Did you bring your camera?" Lindsey seemed completely unfazed by the gathering of insects as she opened the back hatch and pulled out the innertubes.

"Yep. You told me to." Gia grabbed the waterproof pouch that held her phone and adjusted it to dangle just below her chest as she continued to swat at what was probably more imaginary than real insects.

"Good." Lindsey's smile slowly faded. "Um, you okay there?"

"Just trying to shoo the bugs away." She felt like she was in the "before" part of a bug spray commercial, and it was wearing on her nerves. Why did nature have so many flying things in it?

Lindsey placed an innertube on the ground. "Here's yours," she said as she rolled it toward Gia. "We'll put in over there." She pointed to a spot straight ahead.

The innertube wobbled and fell at Gia's feet. The thing looked uncomfortable as hell, and again, she crinkled her face at the thought of stuffing herself in the middle. She huffed as she hopped over it, nestled back into the van, and started to take off her shoes.

"You'll want to keep those on, the rocks can be sharp. Plus, the water's a bit low for this time of the year, so we might have to walk the tubes over the shallow areas."

"These are brand new shoes. If I walk in there, I'll ruin them," Gia scoffed as she continued to unlace her sneakers.

"Trust me, you'll wanna keep them on. We can throw them in Paul's washer when we get back. I think they'll be fine."

"Are you serious?" She glanced at Lindsey in her cute running shorts, tight T-shirt, and cute-as-a-button messy hair. There was no way in hell she was going to wear her expensive tennis shoes in disgusting river water where every form of aquatic life pissed and shit.

"Yeah, I'm serious. Old tennis shoes were on the list of things I suggested you bring," Lindsey said.

While that might have been true, Gia obviously hadn't taken her suggestion seriously. A feeling of incompetence washed over her. "Well, in any case, I think I'll give it a go without them," she said as she tossed her shoes in her tote.

Lindsey shrugged. "Okay, well, um, suit yourself. I guess." She placed a few personal items in a watertight pack and held it out. "Anything you don't want wet, put in here."

"No. I'm good." Gia jingled the waterproof holder around her neck. As she stood, she took one step toward the creek, and started to falter. "Ouch, ouch." She grumbled under her breath as she slowly began maneuvering on the rocks. But each step seemed more agonizing than the last. Between that and the annoying cluster of bugs still hovering around her, her patience was starting to bottom out.

Lindsey lowered herself in the tube. "The water's a little bit chilly at first, but it feels good after a minute. You sure you're okay?"

"I'll…manage." Gia winced with each painful step. She blew out a frustrated breath as she glanced at Lindsey, who had her head tilted back, eyes closed, and seemed to be as peaceful and content as ever. "Okay, fine." Gia huffed as she turned. "Give me a few minutes to put my shoes on."

"Need help?" Lindsey called out.

"Nope, got it." A minute later, she was heading into the water. The shock of the cold took her breath away. "Oh. My. Fucking. God." Gia said through clinched teeth. "Are you kidding me?"

"What?" Lindsey asked. "What's wrong?"

"It's like, what, zero degrees in here, and you want me to submerge my body? Are you insane?" Gia hugged her innertube as she shivered.

Lindsey grinned. "It's not zero degrees. Besides, once you're in, it feels great. I promise." She paddled into deeper water. "Come on, it's really not *that* cold."

"Anything under eighty degrees is cold," Gia snapped.

"Come on. Just take the plunge. I promise, it really is pleasant." Lindsey placed her arms on top of the innertube as the current slowly floated her downstream. "Come on," she called again.

Gia slowly ventured farther out into the river, cursing with each freezing step she took. At this point, she felt like throwing in the towel. Her secret be damned. This was torture, plain and simple, and her tolerance for this type of pain was obviously nonexistent.

"Come on, it's wonderful. You'll see." Lindsey waved.

"Wonderful for corpses maybe, but anyone with a pulse would not agree." Gia scoffed. She shook out another body chill, bent over, and held the tube in place. "Okay Gia," she said in an attempt to embolden herself. "You can do this." She slowly twisted around and ever so gently lowered herself down into the tube. As soon as her butt touched the water, she bolted up. "Holy shit, that's cold," she grumbled as she looked for Lindsey.

She shaded her eyes and squinted downstream. Lindsey waved at her like an enthusiastic child having the time of their life. "Good God, she's so adorable," Gia muttered as her shoulders sank. Oh, stop thinking about sex when you should be plotting your escape, she scolded herself as she weighed her options.

She could just walk out of the river and wait until Lindsey finished floating, whenever that would be. But then again, standing outside a locked car and being eaten alive by bugs wasn't the most appealing. She took a deep breath, held it, and reluctantly lowered herself. This time, instead of sitting, she stiffened like a board and lay on top of the tube. Ha. She smiled in triumph; two could play at this game.

Lindsey paddled upstream. "What are you doing?"

"It's just too damn cold to put my ass in the water." Just concentrate on getting through this morning, she reminded herself. Then she could hibernate at Paul's until Stacy arrived.

"There's some small rapids around the next bend. You'll have much more control if you sit in the tube. You might flip over like that. Your center of gravity is all off."

"Did you say a waterfall is coming up?" Gia craned her neck and looked at Lindsey with alarm.

"No, I said there's some small rapids."

"Well, I don't care what they are, I'm not putting my ass in the water. It's too fucking cold." Did Gia look stupid with her body stiff across the top of an inner tube? Probably. Were her muscles already aching from the strain she was putting on them? Absolutely. Did she care? Not really.

She closed her eyes again and closed herself off to further conversation. She needed to clear her mind of all things Lindsey. The more she interacted with her, the more irritated she became. Lindsey had not only pulled her out of her hibernation, she had also pulled out dormant feelings of desire. And as far as Gia was concerned, both needed to go right back to where they came from. She placed her index finger on her thumb, inhaled, and let out several long breaths.

"Please tell me that's you letting out air and not your tube," Lindsey said.

Annoyed at the interruption, Gia turned her head and opened an eye. "If you must know, I'm trying to meditate the cold out of my body."

"I see. Well, you might want to put that on hold. We're approaching the rapids, and your best bet is to steer down the middle. These are pretty easy ones, and since the river's so low right now, these should be a piece of cake. But you need to follow my lead and do exactly as I do."

Gia craned her neck to get a better view. The rapids didn't look *that* bad. But still, she should probably get farther to the left like Lindsey had and stay behind her. But she was cold, and her muscles were aching, so skillfully maneuvering anywhere and staying stiff was challenging. Instead of following Lindsey's lead, she opted to let the water guide her course.

As the current began picking up speed, Gia watched Lindsey paddle harder and steady her tube between two small boulders. Lindsey whooped and laughed as the current flushed her through the rapids and deposited her into calm waters.

Well, that doesn't look that difficult, Gia thought as she followed. "See," she said smugly. "Piece of cake." But right before she entered the rapids, she hit a cross current. "No, no, no," she called out as the world spun around her.

"You're too far to the left," Lindsey yelled. "Get over more." She waved frantically.

Gia dug her fingers into the rubber and began squealing as the tube accelerated.

"Hold on," Lindsey screamed.

Gia's squeals reached an opera pitch as her tube began bucking and dipping in the turbulent water. She shut her eyes to combat the nausea. The water felt like icicles stabbing at her body. So much pain, so much spinning. Her life began flashing before her eyes. When was the torture going to end?

"Gia?" Lindsey said in a soft voice. "Um, you can open your eyes now. You've been kinda idling for a bit."

She popped her eyes open and blinked at clear blue sky. Other than being completely drenched, she was still miraculously perched on top her tube. "Get me off this river, now!"

Lindsey hooked her legs under Gia's tube and paddled them over to the shore. "Okay, I think we're shallow enough."

Gia rolled off and tried to stand, but her muscles were locked up from straining. As soon as she took a step toward shore, she did a faceplant in the water. She twisted and sat chest-deep in the river and lost control of her temper. "Could this day get any worse?"

"I'm sorry." Lindsey stood and extended her hand.

Gia glared. She didn't want help. She wanted to get off this god-forsaken river, go back to Paul's, and forget this horrible morning had ever happened. In fact, she would love to forget about the past twenty-four hours. She knew leaving Phoenix and coming out here would be a disaster. It was time to renegotiate the terms of their agreement. She huffed as she stood and once again lost her balance.

Lindsey gently wrapped her arms around Gia to steady her. "I've got you," she whispered.

"Um." An unexpected jolt of pleasure surged through Gia as she felt Lindsey's nipples press against hers. "I'm, uh..." she mumbled as Lindsey gently rubbed up and down her back. Gia's knees began to buckle as she thought about those same hands gently rubbing the front of her instead. *Oh my God, get a fucking grip. You are not going there.* She leaned out of the embrace as she shook the fantasy from her head. "You can, um, you can let go now. I think I'm good."

"You sure?" Lindsey said in a soft whisper as she slowly lowered her arms.

"Mm-hmm" The warmth from Lindsey's touch had been nice. Too nice, actually. She couldn't remember the last time she'd felt such a gentle and caring embrace. She could get use to that...wait, what? No. She stepped back. "Take me back to Paul's. Now, Lindsey."

"We're pretty far downstream. It wouldn't be an easy walk back to the car."

Gia huffed in frustration as she stomped to the bank, sat, and tried to rub the warmth she had just felt from the embrace back into her body. "Then what do you suggest?" The muscles in her jaw tightened as her teeth started to chatter.

"Look, it's not much farther to the Non-Float Float Stop. Let's stop for lunch like we planned, and then see if we can catch a ride with someone back to the van."

Gia looked up river, then down. "How much farther?"

Lindsey blew out a breath and scrubbed her hand through her hair. "Based on the pace of the current, I'd say another fifteen minutes or so."

Fifteen minutes! Gia didn't know the rate at which a body could freeze to death, but fifteen minutes seemed like it was in the zone. "Fine." She grabbed her tube, and trudged back into the water. "Well, let's go. The sooner I get off this river, the better," she said through chattering teeth as she tried to mentally block the slap of the cold water on her skin. "Hopefully, the restaurant will be nice and toasty. I need to dry off and warm up."

Lindsey splashed her way into the water. "Yeah, about the restaurant," she said in a soft, almost apologetic voice.

Gia had her arms folded tightly across her chest. "What about it?"

"Well, um, it's not exactly..."

"Exactly what?"

"Well." Lindsey hesitated. "It's kinda an outdoor dining experience. With picnic benches."

Gia let out a heavy sigh. Of course it was. Because a nice normal indoor restaurant with warm air was apparently too much to ask for. She lowered her head. "Well," she said as she wrapped her arms tighter around her chest. "At least it'll be dry."

Fifteen minutes later, they rounded a bend, and off to the right was a cove-like area of still water. A food truck was parked on a section of the rocky shore not much bigger than the vehicle itself. Two people inside moved around each other in perfect synchronicity. A dozen benches were sticking out of the water. People in inner tubes were bellied up to the tables, eating sandwiches, french fries, and chips. A middle-aged woman dressed in fishing waders carried paper plates of food from the truck to the tables.

"Don't even tell me that's—"

"The Non-Float Float Stop, yep." Lindsey smiled.

She pinched the bridge of her nose. "We're not getting out of the tubes and off the river, are we?"

"Well, the whole experience is to be served while you're in your tube, but I guess you could go ashore and stand next to that small patch of rock by the truck and eat your lunch."

"Great." Gia snarled. "Just fucking great."

"Come on," Lindsey said. "It really is kinda fun."

Gia scrubbed her face. Eating lunch while sitting on a block of ice would never be her definition of fun.

"Come on." Lindsey paddled to one of the empty tables. "You'll like it. I know you will."

Within seconds, the server approached. "We have ham and cheese, veggie deluxe, or turkey and cheese on wheat or white roll and your choice of chips or fries."

"I'll have the veggie deluxe on the wheat roll with chips," Lindsey said.

"Same," Gia grumbled. "And please tell me you have coffee or some equally hot beverage."

"We shut the coffee machine down an hour ago."

"I'll pay you for an entire pot if you fire it back up. In fact, I'll pay you double." Hell, she wanted to add, you don't even have to put coffee in it. Hot water will work just fine.

"She's from Phoenix," Lindsey said.

"Ah. Well, that explains the blue lips. I'll get that coffee right away. Cream and sugar?"

"Yes," Gia said as she rubbed her arms. "And please make sure the coffee is hot. As in really hot."

The server nodded, then looked to Lindsey. "You want coffee too?"

"Nah, water's fine."

"Okay, I'll get that right out to ya." The server shuffled over to the food truck and talked to the guy inside in an animated way as she pointed toward Gia.

They sat in silence for the next five minutes as Gia tried to size Lindsey up. She seemed kind, articulate, and cute as hell. Gia wondered what had made her stoop to blackmail? Why would someone so put together threaten to ruin her life? Gia snorted. *Lindsey isn't threatening to ruin your life. It was in shambles long before she even came on the scene.*

Gia frowned at the thought as the server came back with a large mug of coffee. "Here you go, honey, I gave you the biggest mug I could find. You look like you need to take the chill off, so I'll keep the refills coming." She placed the mug, a glass of cream, and several sugar packs on the table.

"Thank you." Gia said as her fingers wrapped around the mug so fast, she felt like an octopus grabbing its prey. The warmth surged through her body. She took several sips and welcomed the hot liquid as it rapidly began melting the ice in her veins.

"Better?" Lindsey asked.

Gia slowly nodded as she cradled the mug and placed it on her chest.

"You have to admit. This is kind of a cool little place," Lindsey said.

Gia's first thought was to make a snarky reply, but the combination of coffee and sun began warming her bones and thawing her temper. She began noticing her surroundings for the first time since she'd walked into the water. Clumps of people were floating, laughing, and having a good time, and the area was lush with vegetation. She reluctantly had to admit that the setting was actually postcard perfect. With a heavy sigh, she glanced at Lindsey, who smiled back at her. Her beautiful blue eyes glistened in the sun. "Yeah," Gia mumbled as she nodded. "I guess it is."

The server came back carrying a tray of food in one hand and the coffeepot in the other. "Here you go, ladies," she said as she refilled Gia's mug. "Let me know if there's anything else I can get you. Enjoy."

Lindsey set one of the plates in front of Gia. She reached for her sandwich, but Lindsey stopped her. "Don't you want to take a picture first? You know, for your article?"

"Oh right. The article." She was so self-consumed with misery, she had completely forgotten she was there to write a positive piece on the gems of Jacobe. She took several pictures of their lunch, then snapped a few of the food truck and surrounding tables. "That should cover it," she said as she fired off several more of the river, returned the phone, and grabbed her sandwich. She took a big bite and hadn't realized how hungry she was until that moment. "Oh wow. This is really good."

"Yeah. It's the best sandwich of the three," Lindsey mumbled as she chewed.

Gia took another sip of coffee and let out a content sigh. *Thank God for small pleasures.* She tore open her bag of chips. As she shoved a few in her mouth, she glanced at Lindsey, who was grinning as if she didn't have a care in the world. She wondered again what her story was.

"What are you thinking?" Lindsey asked.

"Nothing really." Gia shifted the attention back to Lindsey. "You really like living here, huh?"

"In Jacobe? Yeah, I mean, it's where I was born and raised, so I don't really know anything else." Lindsey shrugged.

"I, um, I had an offer that would have put me in southern California after college, but I had to turn it down."

"Oh yeah. Whereabouts?" Gia loved California and had spent many vacations driving up and down the Pacific Coast Highway, stopping at quaint beach communities and wishing she had enough money to live there.

"San Luis Obispo."

"Oh wow, I love San Luis. Why'd you turn it down?" Gia mumbled as she chewed.

"My dad died right before I was about to move, and that would have left my mom all alone. She suffered from Alzheimer's. My, uh, my parents were much older when they had me. I think they blew through all their savings raising me because there wasn't enough left to put Mom in a good memory care facility. So I had to make a decision. My mom or my career."

Gia noticed what looked like a deep sadness in Lindsey's eyes. She couldn't imagine having to make that decision. Her parents had more than enough money to cover an expense like that, should it ever arise. But if they didn't have the funds, would she give up her life to take care of them? She liked to think the answer would be yes, but the fact that she would probably never have to find out gave her a guilty sense of relief. "That had to have been a tough decision."

Lindsey nodded. "I reasoned it away by convincing myself that once Mom passed, I could pick up where I left off, head out to California, and finally start the life I always thought I wanted. But Mom lived way longer than anyone expected. Almost fourteen years longer, to be exact. She died a few months ago."

"I'm so sorry."

Lindsey shrugged.

"Does that mean you're California-bound now?" San Luis Obispo wasn't that far from Phoenix. The thought of having Lindsey closer to her sent an unexpected tingle through her stomach.

Lindsey shook her head. "No, that dream is long gone."

"Why?" Gia tried not to sound disappointed as she took another bite.

"Why?" Lindsey snorted as she repeated the question. "You know, that word has really come up a lot lately. I've asked myself more than once, why not just pick up and go? Why not get back the career that I always wanted?" She frowned. "I guess the truth is because too much life has passed me by. And not only that, the life that I was so anxious to leave has become…comfortable."

Gia stared at Lindsey. *Comfortable*, a word that had haunted her for years. The self-induced isolation that had become her life for the past five years had become debilitatingly comfortable. So much so that dysfunction was her new norm. She no longer even questioned it. It had become so familiar to her, she couldn't see beyond the massive space it was taking up in her life. *Comfortable*. Yeah, she knew that word well.

"Um…" Lindsey trailed off. "Can I ask you something, if you don't mind?"

Uh-oh, here it comes, Gia thought. The glaring question she knew Lindsey was dying to ask about: why she had been faking *Gia's Gems*.

"Is writing all you've ever wanted to do? Or at one point in your life, did you want to do something else?"

Gia exhaled a sigh of relief. "I pretty much always wanted to be a writer." Phew, she really didn't feel like explaining herself right then. "But it didn't pay enough to justify quitting my day job until recently. And that's only because I was fortunate enough to pick up a few mainstream publications who wanted content. The extra money allowed me to finally become a full-time writer." Even though the pictures in *Gia's Gems* were Stacy's, the writing was all hers, and it was an accomplishment that she was extremely proud of.

"Oh yeah? What was your day job?"

"I created instructional videos for a healthcare conglomerate. At the beginning of each week, they would send me a script, and by the end of that week, I sent them a full video with voiceover, music, and graphics. They let me telecommute, which was nice because it allowed me to set my own hours and pace."

"Wow, that actually sounds kinda cool."

Gia shrugged "Boring is the more appropriate word." There was nothing fulfilling about producing instructional videos. The job had been no more than a paycheck. And even though she was making only a fraction of what she'd once made, she was so much more fulfilled. And that alone was worth the difference in pay.

The server announced their bill was sixteen forty-five and that the coffee was on the house. Lindsey had money in hand before Gia could get her pouch unclipped.

"You didn't need to pay for mine," Gia protested.

Lindsey waved her off. "The least I could do since it's clear you're hating this day."

Gia opened her mouth to disagree, then closed it. It was true. She did hate the day. But right now, with hot coffee melting her frozen bones and the sun warming her skin, she was having an unexpectedly nice moment. The old Gia would have loved every single minute of this day. She would have laughed at herself while spinning down the rapids, embraced the surrounding beauty, and enjoyed the company of an attractive woman. The new Gia was just bitching her way through it all. She frowned. *What happened to me?*

"Well." Lindsey turned. "There's a path through those trees that will take us to the road. We can try and flag someone down and ask if they could give us a ride to the car."

Gia followed Lindsey's finger to a thick clump of foliage. Between hiking through the woods and trying to hitch a ride with strangers or freezing her ass off and just finishing the float, she was leaning toward floating. "How far to the shuttle service?"

"That's downstream a bit. If we float with the current, we'll be there in about an hour, but if we paddle, we can easily knock off ten to fifteen minutes."

"I'm, um…" She took a deep breath as she steadied her nerves. She glanced at Lindsey, then back to the trail that led into the dense foliage. "I'm actually feeling better now. So, um, why don't we just let the current take us to the place that has the shuttle?" She might regret the decision, but between the options, it definitely seemed to have the safer outcome.

"Really?" Lindsey beamed.

"Yeah. I mean, I lost feeling in my extremities a while ago so what's another hour?" Gia said with a slight smile. Why continue to struggle through a moment that was quickly turning into something she was finding pleasurable?

"There's a beautiful area over the next bend where a bunch of birds hang out. It'll be an awesome spot for a photo, and a ton of turtles sunbathe on the tree limbs and rocks that stick out of the river, and…"

As Gia watched Lindsey's animated speech, she felt a twinge in her heart. Not so much for Lindsey—although that was definitely there—but more for a distant memory that reminded her of her own passion for life. A flame extinguished years ago for all the wrong reasons. The collateral damage of a breakup that she'd allowed to decimate not only her heart but the many feelings she stored in that little beating muscle. She had become someone who was bitter, party of one. She smiled at the catchphrase Stacy said from time to time. "At least tell me there are no more rapids," she said as she pushed away from the table.

Lindsey paddled over. "Um, well, maybe just one more. But no bigger than the one we already came down, and now that you're sitting, you won't have any issues. The proven method always works best."

Gia smiled but didn't bother to reply as she closed her eyes and leaned her head back to let the afternoon sun bathe her with warmth. What had started out as the shittiest day ever was shaping up to be halfway enjoyable. Well, maybe halfway was too generous; more like somewhat enjoyable. She opened an eye and glanced over. *Well played, Lindsey, well played.*

An hour and a half later, they were headed back to Paul's. They had dry clothes on and to-go lattes in hand. And with the beauty of the Midwest in all its green glory surrounding her, Gia was beginning to feel a crack in the Audrey-apocalyptic-armor she'd put on years ago and had never taken off. She glanced at Lindsey, who was bobbing her head and lightly tapping her fingers on the steering wheel. Lindsey was really beautiful in that organic tomboy kind of way. Had they met under different circumstances, she would have definitely seen the potential for a relationship.

She stared out the window as she chuckled at the absurdity of that thought when her phone rang. "Hi, Mom, is everything okay with Brody?"

"Everything is fine with my little muffin head. It's your father that you need to worry about."

"What'd Dad do now?"

"Where to begin. He pressed the wrong button on the computer again, and apparently, we are now the proud owners of a hundred gecko statues from Valley Garden and Supply. He says he was trying to buy me one for the rose garden, and the computer just went haywire and put in two extra zeros."

Gia rubbed her forehead as she let out a sigh. "Computers don't go haywire like that."

"Gia said it's user error, Henry," her mom screamed, and Gia jerked the phone away from her ear. "Is there any way you can correct this, dear? I had your father sign a note that says he isn't allowed to touch the computer unsupervised anymore."

"I bet that went over well." She smiled. If her dad really did sign the note, she knew he had no intention of ever honoring the agreement. But that was the dance of her parents.

"That's a story for another day. Anyway, how're you getting along?"

"I, uh." Gia glanced at Lindsey, who had a slight smile on her face as she kept her eyes on the road. She felt like saying she was getting along surprisingly well. That the person she had been dreading being with wasn't as god-awful as she'd made her out to be. In fact, just the opposite. "Good, everything's good."

"Ha!" Again, Gia jerked the phone away from her head. "I knew that once you got out of this phase you'd be back to your old self."

"I wasn't in a…never mind." This wasn't the time or place to have another argument with her mom over the many phases of her life. "In fact, I need to get going. I'll call and have the order reprocessed to one statue." This wasn't the first time she had to call a store and change an order her father had messed up, and she was sure it wasn't going to be the last. "Kiss Brody for me, and I'll call you soon." Gia hung up. "Um, excuse me while I make a call on my father's behalf."

Lindsey nodded. "No worries, do what you need to do." She sipped her coffee, and when Gia finally hung up again, Lindsey said, "Everything okay?"

"With the order for one hundred gecko statues, yes. With my parents, no. I think it's fair to conclude that they've never really been okay. Sometimes I wonder how and why they remain married." One day, her parents could be laughing and loving toward the other, and the next, they weren't on speaking terms. The stomach-churning roller-coaster ride of her childhood had become somewhat entertaining now that she was an adult. *Funny how normal a toxic situation can look once you've been around it long enough.*

"Relationships can be…" Lindsey paused as she cocked her head. "Interesting."

"That's a loaded word." Gia thought about her parents and then reflected on her own past relationships. *It's no wonder my love life is a wreck with role models like that.*

Lindsey nodded. "I guess it is. Um, I assume since *Gia's Gems* is all about a single woman finding the gay gems in small towns, you're not in a relationship?"

Gia snorted and shook her head. "Nope, not even close. You?"

"Single as well," Lindsey answered in a tone that carried a recognized hint of bitterness.

"Well, here's to singlehood." She raised her cup even though she still held hope that one day she would be in a loving relationship. To share in the passions of lovemaking and the comforts of cohabitation. For the long haul, she optimistically added as she tilted her cup toward Lindsey's. Because the short sprint relationships she seemed to keep getting involved in not only sucked, they were exhausting.

❖

"Touché." Lindsey smiled as she touched her cup to Gia's. A familiar pain settled in her heart. Being single was never something she'd wanted to be. It was just something that had happened to her. Like her dad's death, turning down the opportunity to move to California, and her mom's Alzheimer's. *For once, it'd be nice if something positive actually happened. Is that too much to ask?*

Twenty minutes later, she pulled up to Paul's and grabbed Gia's tote. "Here you go." She extended her arm as Gia slid out of her seat, arched her back, and turned.

"Thanks." Gia took the bag and flung it on her shoulder.

"I was thinking. Later tonight, I'll be at Masquerades, Jacobe's one and only gay bar. It's not too far from here, and I think I owe you a drink for being such a good sport out on the river." She grinned in the hope that Gia would accept.

"I um…I'll think about it."

"Oh, okay," she said, disappointed. "Well, you have my number." She lingered and nibbled her lip. She contemplated giving Gia a hug and telling her that she'd had a nice day and that being on the river brought back fond memories of her parents. Memories that had been blurred with time. But as she stood there staring in awkward silence, she began second-guessing herself. Was it too soon for an affectionate embrace? They really hadn't hit it off right out of the gate, but there had been a few moments on the river where she'd sensed Gia was checking her out. Was the ice between them thawing? Lindsey knew a hug could answer a lot of nagging questions because there was a big difference between a *see you around* hug and an *I want to get to know you better* hug. And right now, she wanted to convey to Gia that she really wanted to get to know her better.

Oh God, Gia thought, please tell me you're not thinking about hugging me good-bye. Under any other circumstances, she would accept. The day that had started out as one of her all-time least favorites had ended up in a rather delightful way. She'd actually enjoyed listening to Lindsey's stories about her childhood on the river. Yes, normally, she would have wrapped Lindsey in her arms and given her a hug that signaled she'd not only had a nice day, but she might like to get to know her better. Unfortunately, there was a lingering fishy smell that she was convinced was emanating from her armpits, and the only thing she wanted touching her body was the warm water from a shower. As for going out this evening, she just wanted to relax in her bed with a book and a glass of wine. Baby steps, Gia thought as the desire to return to being a hermit kicked in. Baby steps.

"Well, um," Lindsey said as she backed away. "I guess I should be going. Hopefully, you'll think about coming out tonight."

"Yep, okay, I will." Gia nodded as she turned. "And, Lindsey," she said over her shoulder.

"Yeah?"

"Thank you. The morning was…" She paused in search of the right words. "Unexpectedly pleasant." From the corner of her eye, she saw Lindsey smile and fist-bump the air. Gia chuckled at the adorable way Lindsey expressed herself. "Mmm," she moaned as she stepped inside, lifted her head, and sniffed the air like a dog. "What am I smelling?"

"Apple pies, I just pulled them out of the oven. I sell them to Masquerades, but I always keep one back for the house." Paul walked out from the kitchen as he rubbed his hands on a red-checkered kitchen towel.

"They smell wonderful."

"Taste even better. How was the river?" He asked.

"Cold," was all Gia said as she walked to the stairs and started to climb. A warm shower was calling to her, and she really wanted to be alone.

"Sounds like you had a miserable day."

Gia stopped on the third step. She wanted to say in a dry tone that putting one's ass in a tube and floating down a cold river had never been on her bucket list. But as she opened her mouth, Lindsey's adorable smiling face and the feel of her gentle hands flashed in her mind. She thought of the warmth of the coffee, the beauty of the foliage, and the moments when she was so engaged with Lindsey that she'd actually felt like her old self. "Actually…" She smiled as she cocked her head. "You know what, the day wasn't half-bad."

"Well, all right then." He smiled and shuffled back into the kitchen.

Well, all right then, she thought as she headed to her room. Two days down, three to go, and by this time tomorrow, she could pass the baton to Stacy. Then bye-bye, Jacobe, hello, home.

"You've got this," she whispered to herself as she entered her room and headed to the shower. But as she let the mix of warm water and lavender soap soothe and relax her, her thoughts drifted again to Lindsey. She closed her eyes as she covered her breasts in suds and envisioned Lindsey's hands as her own. She gently stroked her nipples as a shiver tingled up her body. It had been too long, and the thought of having shower sex was turning her on. She pinched her erect nipples and moaned in delight. She could easily pleasure herself right now; it wouldn't take much. Just a little bit of pressure on the right spot would do it, she thought as she slowly slid her hand down her stomach. But before she reached her clit, she stopped. She leaned against the tile, tilted her face to the showerhead, and let the water rain down on her. She inhaled the steam and exhaled frustration. She was getting tired of pleasuring herself. She wanted to feel another woman's hands caressing and stroking her in all the right places. And she wanted to be talked to in all the sexy and exciting ways lovers did while in bed together.

She sighed as she shut the water off and grabbed a towel. What she wanted was Lindsey.

CHAPTER SEVEN

Gia sat on the porch swing, gently rocking as she relaxed beneath the moonlight. The sound of insects filled the air, and the mesmerizing dance of fireflies played out in front of her. The air, although still thick, lacked the intensity of the day's humidity, and it was actually quite pleasant. Her gaze was far away as she sat back and replayed a few moments from the morning. "I really have nothing to complain about," she said in a soft voice as she thought about Lindsey. Although Gia had portions of her life that felt like they were spinning out of control, she'd always had a career, money, and the luxury of changing her direction anytime she wanted. Three things Lindsey had never had. She wondered how different her life would be if the shoe was on the other foot when she heard the creak of the screen door, and soft footsteps approached.

"It's a beautiful night, huh?" Paul stepped onto the porch and tilted his head toward the sky.

"It is. Paul, I don't mean to sound like a city girl, but what am I hearing?"

He sat next to her. "Those are cicadas and crickets. Loud little fuckers, aren't they?" he said in a playful way.

As long as they don't get near me, I'm good with them, she thought as she nodded. "I'm just not used to hearing anything but cars, sirens, and planes."

He crinkled his nose. "That sounds just awful."

She chuckled. "Guess it's all about what you're used to."

"True." He paused. "What brings you out on the patio tonight?"

"Just…thinking." She didn't offer any other information as a comfortable silence fell between them while she listened to the sounds of the night. This town was starting to get to her in a surprisingly good way. In just forty-eight hours, she was feeling more normal than during any therapy session she'd had in the past five years. Maybe it was being in nature and out of the concrete jungle that was thawing her isolation freeze, or maybe it was being in a town with a vibe so homey and quaint, it beckoned her to be a part of it. Or maybe it was because of the woman who was currently taking up a lot of real estate in her mind and making her feel all the exciting things a heart felt when it began to share its beat for someone else.

Paul nodded. "Well, for what it's worth, Linds said she had a great day on the river with you." He grinned.

"Did she?" Gia was pleasantly taken aback.

"Yep."

"What's her story, if you don't mind me asking?" What she really wanted to ask was, why was someone who seemed so amazingly wonderful not in a relationship?

He smiled. "I've known Lindsey pretty much my whole life. She's a year older than I am. I always say she fulfills the older sister role in my life, and I like to think I fulfill the younger brother in hers." He paused as he looked down. "When I was sixteen, my parents caught me kissing another boy. They promptly disowned me and threw me out of the house. Lindsey was the one who came swooping in with all her glory and saved me. She talked her parents into taking me in, and they set up a room in their basement for me so I wouldn't be on the streets."

"Oh, Paul, I'm so sorry."

He waved her off. "It's okay, I'm over it. Things worked out in the end. I have a fabulous business and an even more fabulous husband. I also have people in this town who'd be there for me in a heartbeat, Linds being at the top of that list. That's why I was by her side when Jasmine broke her heart."

"Her ex?"

"Not just an ex, *the* ex. Her high school friend turned lover turned lying bitch. Three years after they got together, Jasmine decided to replace being gay with religious righteousness, and she dumped Lindsey for a guy she barely knew. Then, to top it off, she told everyone that the reason she and Lindsey were no longer friends was because Lindsey was doing drugs. Which was a total lie, but a lot of people around here believed it."

"Wow." Gia thought about Audrey and the betrayal she'd felt when Audrey had an affair. That was bad enough. She couldn't imagine what it would have been like if Audrey had also tried to turn people against her.

"Yeah, wow. That gossip flew with wings around this town, and it devastated Lindsey's parents. She had to correct that bullshit really fast because they were about to yank her from college."

"Did she tell them the truth?"

"No. She was still in love with Jasmine and didn't want to hurt her because that's the kind of person Lindsey is." He turned. "Anyway, her parents let her finish her senior year when Linds told them it was all just an unfortunate misunderstanding. Jasmine ended up marrying that guy, and a year later, they moved to Baton Rouge. No one's heard from her since. Good riddance, I say, but poor Linds was never the same. She's had some tough breaks."

"She told me a little about her dad dying and the job offer in California."

"I pitched in as much as possible to help with her mom. It was just sad all the way around." He got up and brushed off the back of his jeans, then glanced at Gia. "Linds is one in a million. The girl's got a heart of gold. And speaking of, I'm heading over to Masquerades, to meet up with her and Jenn for a drink, care to join?"

"Who's Jenn?" she asked as a touch of jealousy reared up.

"Her best friend and the town's most amazing hair stylist. She owns Cuts and Curls, off Stark Street, and let me tell you, that girl's got the gift." He held out his hands, palms up. "Come with me as my date tonight."

"No, thanks, I think I'll just hang here for the evening." It would be nice to see Lindsey again, but she was a little embarrassed about the way she'd been acting. She still didn't excuse the blackmail, but she was definitely excusing the blackmailer.

"Come on, a fun night on the town with yours truly? Please tell me what else you have going on that could possibly top that."

"I…" Gia trailed off in thought. She had taken a late afternoon nap, and she was actually feeling quite refreshed, so she couldn't use fatigue as an excuse. But going to bars had never that appealing, even before she'd closed herself off to the world.

"It's a cute little place, and they have a drink called the Long Island Hula that makes you want to get up and dance. Or maybe that's just me."

"Paul…"

"Come on, one drink, and we're back here swapping more stories, I promise."

She chuckled. "Oh, all right. Let me go grab my purse." She pushed off the bench and shuffled into the house. "One drink and that's all, you promise?" She called over her shoulder.

"On my beautiful husband's body." He made a scout's honor sign.

A minute later, she was back on the porch, purse in hand, ready to go. "Lead the way, Romeo."

"This is going to be so much fun. Come on." He wrapped his arm around her. "We can walk it in fifteen minutes. This way, if we get a little tipsy, we won't be behind a wheel."

Gia stopped walking. "You said one drink." She really wasn't in the mood for a long night in a bar. The thought of being around a crowd was still a bit unnerving, and although she felt at ease around Paul, she was still way out of her comfort zone. Especially around Lindsey.

"Yes, but I never said anything about not making that one drink a double." He laughed as they strolled down the street.

As they approached Masquerades, Gia instantly regretted agreeing to go out. From the outside, the place looked like a total sleezy bar, and she had been to enough gay dives to last a lifetime. One quick drink, she told herself, then I'm outta here. But as soon as Paul opened the door, she was pleasantly surprised. The place was small and cozy, with a lot of charm and character. Exposed brick and dark mahogany wood with open ventilation gave it a loft feel. The lighting was classy and strategically positioned. The wall to her left was the bar, with floor to ceiling mirrors that showcased an impressive collection of bottles. Against the other wall were stainless steel coffee machines, a display case full of baked goods, and a limited food menu chalked on a board. She instantly felt comfortable.

"There they are." Paul's arm shot up as he acknowledged someone waving him over to a booth. "I brought a plus one, hope you don't mind." He said as he sat next to the waving woman, presumably Jenn, which gave Gia no choice but to slide in next to Lindsey.

She would have preferred a table where they could have all sat a comfortable distance apart, but as she looked around, she noticed every other booth, table, and comfy overstuffed chair was taken. She glanced at Lindsey, and her pulse quickened, and her palms started sweating. In just forty-eight hours, Lindsey had managed to do something Gia hadn't been able to do in the past five years: make her start to feel like her old self again.

They ordered drinks, and Lindsey introduced Gia to Jenn.

Jenn extended her hand. "Nice to finally meet you."

"Finally?" Gia cocked her hand.

"Lindsey's been talking you up for some time. She's been a huge fan of your writing for a while."

"Really?" Gia arched a brow and beamed. "A huge fan, huh?" She was proud of *Gia's Gems*, and the fact that Lindsey was a fan was a recognition that meant something to her. Audrey had never acknowledged or sung her praises for anything she did. And after a while, it had destroyed her self-esteem and replaced it with self-doubt. It was hard to take joy in anything she accomplished when the end result was never celebrated.

"Well, yeah." Lindsey cleared her throat. "I mean, you're a great writer, and you can really bring these cute little towns to life in such a vivid and witty way. It really made me want to visit many of them." Lindsey smiled as she averted her eyes.

"Which we're hoping will be the outcome with Jacobe after your article comes out," Paul said.

"That's the plan." Gia said.

"Long Island Hula for you." The server placed the extra-large drink in front of Paul. "And a light on tap for you." She slid the beer in front of Gia. "Anything else?"

"I think we're good for now," Jenn said before she turned to Gia. "You should probably get a picture of Paul's drink before he devours it. Masquerades is kinda known for their Long Island Hulas."

"Oh, um. Yeah. Sure." Gia snapped a few shots, then slid out of the booth and took a few more of the bar and coffee area. She sat and scrolled through the pictures with an approving nod, then gestured to Paul. "I'll need to get some photos of your place tomorrow."

He whipped out his phone. "What's your number?"

"Excuse me?"

"Your number." He jiggled his phone.

Gia hesitated. Giving out her cell number felt like an invasion of privacy. Only friends and family had that number. Well, that wasn't totally true, based on the latest barrage of texts and phone calls from every solicitor and scammer. She reluctantly rattled it off, and seconds later, her phone chimed. There were pictures of Paul standing by his sign, baking in the kitchen, turning down a bed, etc. "Wow, these are so…" She wanted to say *staged*.

"Perfect, yes, I know." He grinned. "When Linds said you were coming, I took the liberty. Jenn did the hair, and Jeff took the pictures."

"Thanks. I'll be sure to include one in the article." Of course, she would. How could she not? Gia thought it was cute that he'd gone to such extremes in the hope of getting mentioned. She tossed the phone in her purse, glanced around the table at everyone, and smiled. She could tell by their conversation that there was a lot of love—and years—shared between them. She sipped her drink as a wave of loneliness washed over her. She was definitely the outsider in this family circle of friends. But as if reading her mind, Lindsey leaned in and began providing the backstory to the latest gossip and inside jokes. And it didn't take long for Gia to feel welcome amongst them.

Two hours later, Paul's one drink promise became three, but instead of being annoyed, Gia was enjoying the evening. Jenn was witty, and Gia found herself amused and entertained with the stories of their adventures. A twinge of envy hit her. True, she had Stacy, but she traveled so much, they rarely got together anymore. Not only that, Stacy lived on the other side of town, which for Phoenix meant an hour or more drive, depending on the traffic. Here, everyone lived in close proximity and could just pop in on each other without having to calculate time of arrival around the city's commuting hours. Just one more thing about small-town living that felt very appealing.

When it was time to go, Gia grabbed the check to mumbled protests around the table. "Please, it's my treat. Thank you for a pleasant evening. I had a really nice time." Now that she had been pulled from her hibernation kicking and screaming, she was finding it rather easy and somewhat enjoyable getting back into the groove of what used to resemble her former life. She glanced at Lindsey. And maybe that had more to do with the company she was keeping than anything else.

They scooted out of the booth, and Paul stumbled a bit. "Did you two walk here?" Lindsey asked with concern in her voice.

"Yes, he wanted to walk in case either of us ended up tipsy," Gia said.

"He passed tipsy two drinks and a hula dance ago. I'll walk you back." Lindsey placed an arm around his waist. "And since I live only a few blocks from him, I'll just jog home."

"Is that safe?" It was late, and the thought of Lindsey walking alone made Gia feel uneasy. Although she lived in what she considered a nice neighborhood in Phoenix, she still wouldn't feel comfortable being out alone this late at night.

Lindsey chuckled. "It's totally safe. One of the perks of living in a small town, I guess." She hugged Jenn as they gathered outside the door. "I'm going to walk these guys home. He's too drunk to navigate."

"Don't be silly, we can all pile in my car."

"No. That's okay. It's, um, it's a nice night for a walk," Lindsey said in a low voice.

Jenn cocked her head. "Since when do you..." Her brows shot up, and a huge grin spread across her face. "Well, it was a pleasure meeting you, Gia. I look forward to catching up some more tomorrow." She headed to her car and waved. "Text me when you get to your house, Linds."

"Tomorrow?" Gia turned to Lindsey.

"Jenn's throwing a barbeque at her house," Lindsey said. "I thought we could hang out there after we get back from a short morning adventure. It'll give you a chance to meet some other people in case you want to pick their brains regarding all things Jacobe. And if not, we can just hang out by Jenn's pool, which you'll be happy to know, is heated."

"Oh, thank God." Gia smiled. Although she wouldn't be opposed to being in another situation where Lindsey had to warm her up.

Lindsey helped prop up Paul's sagging body. "Come on, buddy, let's get you home."

The temperature was low seventies, the moon was bright, and the town was peacefully quiet as they strolled. Gia was enjoying the stillness of the night and felt comfortable in the silence that had fallen between them.

"Um," Lindsey interrupted her thoughts. "Do you mind if I ask you something?"

Here it comes. Gia exhaled. "Sure."

"Regarding *Gia's Gems*. Um, why did you..."

"Lie?"

Lindsey nodded. "Yeah."

Gia sighed. Part of her didn't want to say anything. Explaining something that she recognized as a bit crazy was going to be embarrassing. Being judged by Stacy was one thing, but being judged by someone who she was developing feelings for made her feel uncomfortably exposed.

A litany of excuses for not answering were on the tip of her tongue. But as she gazed into Lindsey's eyes, she saw what appeared to be sadness, as though Lindsey had some sort of emotional stake in her answer.

"I had just gotten out of a five-year relationship with a verbally abusive, egotistical, self-serving woman. Think narcissist on steroids. Her name's Audrey, and she thought she was better than me in every way. Intelligence, looks, job, sex, you name it. Apparently, I was inferior in all those categories. It messed me up a bit, and in the end, I became a shell of the person I once was. Then one day, she told me she was in love with someone else. And that was that."

But Gia knew by the lingering bitter taste of her last words that she still carried anger and resentment toward Audrey. "It was weird. One minute, we're lovers, and the next, we're barely speaking to each other. A few days later, I came home from work to an almost empty house. I was devastated. I withdrew and didn't feel like doing anything with anyone. I became a bit of a recluse, which you have to admit, is pretty easy to do nowadays. Anyway, the months of my isolation turned into years." Gia sighed. "Most of my friends gave up on me, except one, Stacy. She was pretty much the only one who stuck by me. And to her credit, she has always tried to drag me out from my rabbit hole."

"I'm so sorry you had to go through that. Your ex sounds horrible."

"She was. But there were enough moments in the madness that held it together for almost five years. But yeah, overall, it was a rough ride. We're just two different people."

"So how does *Gia's Gems* play into all that?"

"Stacy would send me pictures of all the places she traveled for work, hoping they would entice me to get out there and jumpstart my life. One night, after I'd had a little too much wine, I photoshopped myself into her photos, wrote a fake article, and sent it to her as a joke. The next day, she sent it to a friend of hers at *L Online* as a sample of my writing with the hope that they would hire me. But they loved *Gia's Gems* so much, they wanted to publish it. I was really upset when she told me, but then we both figured, what the hell, the article will run once, no one will be the wiser, and that'll be that."

"Obviously, it wasn't."

"No. *Gia's Gems* really caught on, and the genie became harder and harder to put back in the bottle. And I guess that's on me. I felt so broken that I started embracing a fake life. I no longer knew who I was anymore, and maybe, I just didn't care. By that point, I had even lost the motivation to find myself."

A mixture of anxiety and regret churned in Gia's stomach as she turned to Lindsey. "I didn't mean for it to hurt anyone." She searched Lindsey's eyes for something that said she understood. Even if Lindsey disagreed with her for doing it, she just needed her to understand why.

"Gia, I—"

"Are we home yet?" Paul slurred as he stumbled backward and began to fall.

Gia stepped behind him, reached out, and her arms tangled with Lindsey's. "Easy there." She steadied him but focused on Lindsey. Their bodies were entwined, and once again, the contact ignited all the parts of her that had been dormant since Audrey. "I'll um…" She slowly slid her arms out and repositioned them around Paul. "I'll take this side if you've got that side?" Keep it together, she scolded herself as she took a deep breath to steady her desires. She was only two days out of a five-year hibernation and three days away from saying good-bye to this place. Did she really want to add another layer to her already messed up life?

Yes, actually. She kind of did.

"A girlfriend sandwich." Paul laughed.

"I think someone's going to be a bit hungover in the morning," Lindsey said as they shuffled up the walkway. They maneuvered Paul onto his bed, and by the time they untied his shoes, he was sound asleep.

"Think he'll be okay?" Gia asked.

"Yeah. He'll be fine. Now come on." Lindsey tilted her head toward the kitchen. "I could smell the pie as soon as we walked in." She removed the glass dome that covered the dessert. "Grab two plates." She gestured to the cabinet as she cut into the pie. "Let's eat outside and continue talking."

Gia nodded as she followed Lindsey to the porch and took a seat on the swing. She leaned back and took a moment to appreciate the sky. The blanket of stars was mesmerizing. "The sky is so beautiful," she said in a soft voice as she turned. She wanted to say, *and so are you*, but she cringed and thought the statement was too cheesy.

"Yes, it is." Lindsey smiled, then broke their stare as she took a bite and moaned. "Damn, Paul can make a good apple pie."

"He definitely knows how to cook," Gia said as she sensed a shyness coming from Lindsey. "I bet he would have been a star pupil at a culinary school."

"Yeah, he would have. And at one point in his life, he really wanted to go, but he was never given the chance."

"He told me about being thrown out of his house and coming to live with you." A sadness tugged at her heart. How the hell could a parent do that to their child? As flawed as hers were, at least they embraced her sexuality. Even though her mom considered it a phase, they still stood by her.

"Yeah, my dad and I turned a portion of the basement into a makeshift room for him. When he turned eighteen, he moved into a studio apartment. By then, he was working as a waiter and could afford his own place. Eventually, he crawled his way up the ranks in the restaurant business and made some pretty decent money. He bought this house when it went into foreclosure a few years ago and turned it into the town's only B and B."

"Well, he did a wonderful job on the place," Gia said as she set the plate aside, leaned back, and once again tilted her head toward the sky.

"The house looked like shit when he bought it. I thought he made a big mistake, but he and Jeff really turned it around. Paul had the vision. Jeff had the muscle."

"It's nice that Paul has Jeff. He sounds like the perfect guy," Gia said as she focused on one particular bright star.

"Yeah, it's too bad you won't have a chance to meet him, the two of them really do complement each other."

Complement. Gia scoffed at the word as she turned. "I have never known what it's like to be in a relationship like that."

"I thought I did at one time, but I was wrong," Lindsey said in a soft voice.

Gia glanced at Lindsey. The physical attraction was obvious, but the more they communicated, the more she found herself not only relating to Lindsey but genuinely liking her. She was someone Gia could see herself having a complementary relationship with.

She shook off the thoughts. In a few short days, she would be out of Jacobe, and she would probably never be back. But Lindsey had awoken something in her, and because of that, she would be forever grateful. Now she needed to take her newfound feelings home and find someone local. "Paul told me a little something about your past. Sounds like you've had your share of bad relationships."

"Just the one." Lindsey held up her finger.

"Wait, you mean to tell me you've only been with one woman? Seriously?" She didn't mean to sound so shocked, but someone as beautiful as Lindsey could have her pick.

Lindsey nodded.

Gia smiled. "Holy shit, you're almost a virgin."

"Well. Far from a virgin." Lindsey giggled. "But yeah, I've only been with one."

"Wow." Gia felt like a player as she thought about the fifteen women she had been with. But to be fair—and give her mom a reluctant nod—she'd gone through a phase in college where she took her newfound sexual identity for several test drives.

"Did Paul fill you in on what Jasmine did after she broke up with me?"

"Yeah, kinda. And he also said that you didn't tell anyone."

Lindsey shook her head. "I didn't want to hurt her because I was still in love with her. And, I was hoping that she was still in love with me, and that somehow, we would get back together." She shuffled her feet.

Gia reflected on her breakup with Audrey. Would she have taken Audrey back after everything that happened between them? Yeah, she probably would have. As insane as that sounded, if Audrey would have asked for a second chance in that first, post-breakup year, she would have said yes. She wasn't sure if that was a sign of love or of how completely lost and codependent she had become. "Do you ever want to be in another relationship?" Gia asked more to herself than Lindsey.

"Very much so, but taking care of Mom all these years didn't allow me the opportunity to date. And now that I have the opportunity, I've yet to find the right person." Lindsey waved dismissively. "Maybe it's just not meant to be."

"I know what you mean. Sometimes, I think I never want to be in another relationship ever again. Then I read a lesbian romance novel and end up going to bed with my vibrator, wishing it was a woman."

Lindsey threw her head back and laughed. "Oh my God, you did not just say that."

"Too much information?" Gia laughed. How had this adorable woman turned her life so completely upside down in just a few short days? Such a kindhearted and beautiful soul. Gia sat frozen as her mind raced with the idea to lean in. Everything inside her wanted to kiss Lindsey, to feel the sensation of their lips together, tongues deep in exploration. Yet, there was still that little voice in her head that warned her not to get involved. The reminder that her time in this town, and with Lindsey, was ticking down. But as a surge of sexual energy shot through her, desire overpowered reason. She licked her lips and slowly leaned in.

Paul loudly stumbled onto the porch. "Am I drunk?" He shuffled over, scooted between them, and rested his head on Lindsey's shoulder. "You guys are having girl talk without me, aren't you? And did you get into my pie?" He grabbed a morsel off Gia's plate and shoved it in his mouth.

"How are you even here? You were totally passed out when we put you to bed," Lindsey said in an annoyed tone.

"I had to pee. And when I got up, I realized I was fully clothed." He tugged at his shirt. "I never sleep with my clothes on. And then I heard voices different than the ones in my head, so I followed them out here. And look. Here you are."

He addressed Gia. "Thanks for being my plus one tonight. I had fun."

"Me too." She patted his thigh as she slowly got up. "Now if you'll excuse me, I'll leave you two to enjoy the night. I, uh, I should probably get to bed. It's been a long day."

"You don't have to go," Lindsey said as she gave Gia a look that seemed to plead with her.

The message was received, but Gia was having a hard time settling her mind. She wanted Lindsey so badly right now that the desire was starting to scare her. Her body was tingling with so much sexual intensity, she ached. This was not what she'd planned and not what she wanted. She needed time to think. "No." She faked a yawn. "I really should get to bed. Thanks for such a wonderful evening. It was…" She wanted to say perfect but settled on, "Nice."

"Okay." Paul lifted his hand and waved a floppy good-bye. "She's so nice," he mumbled as Gia grabbed for the screen door.

She glanced back. Lindsey was looking at her with puppy dog eyes, and for a moment, she felt the urge to close the distance, cup Lindsey's face in her hands, and kiss her long and hard. She didn't want to let the magic of the evening go, and the look in Lindsey's eyes seemed to be conveying the same thoughts. She loosened her grip on the screen door and began to take a step, but Paul pulled Lindsey into a bear hug.

"I love my Lindsey girl," he said as he squeezed her.

Gia smiled. She lowered her head, let out a frustrated breath, and went inside. She took a moment to steady herself as she leaned against the wall. A gleam of hope that Lindsey would come barreling through the door and kiss her flashed through her mind. She held that thought as she waited. But as soon as Lindsey and Paul started talking about their high school days, she pushed off the wall and slowly walked up the stairs to a bed she wanted to share with the most amazing woman she'd met in a long time. She let out a long sigh as she entered her room and back-kicked the door shut.

❖

Lindsey could barely concentrate on what Paul was babbling about. Everything inside her wanted to rush into the house, pull Gia onto her bed, and make love to her. She squirmed on the bench as she thought of touching her. Damn. It'd been a long time since she'd had such a strong reaction. Good to know all her parts were still working but frustrating as hell that she couldn't act on it.

"I'm going to miss her when she leaves." Paul's statement brought Lindsey back to the conversation.

"I'll miss her too." Lindsey exhaled. It wasn't just Gia. She would also miss the feelings now coming from her body as it emerged from its hibernation. Feelings she hadn't felt since Jasmine. Oh, well. Her shoulders sagged as she glanced at Paul. It wasn't like any of that mattered. The fact was, the two of them came from different worlds, and in a few short days, those worlds would no longer overlap. The only thing that would still linger between them was a nice friendship. And while friendships could be wonderful and long-lasting, Lindsey wanted more from Gia. She had been reserving a spot in her life for someone her heart recognized as a soulmate. And maybe that someone could be Gia.

"I like her, Linds." Paul rested his head on her shoulder.

Lindsey squirmed. She was wet and aroused and uncomfortable. "Yeah," she whispered as she pulled at her jeans. "I like her too."

CHAPTER EIGHT

Lindsey sat with Paul at the kitchen island, drinking coffee, when Gia came bounding into the room.

"Am I late?" She placed her jacket on the kitchen counter, and leaned against it.

"Not at all." Lindsey smiled as her gaze rolled over Gia and her pulse quickened. She wanted to close the distance between them and greet her with a passionate morning kiss, but the intimate line still hadn't been crossed, and permission hadn't been granted. Thanks a lot, Paul, she playful snarled in her head. "I came a little early and brought coffee." She handed Gia a cup. "I figured Paul might not be in the best shape to make his own this morning."

He placed his elbows on the counter, hunched over his cup, and started rubbing his temples. "You guys, I feel like shit. Why didn't one of you come to my rescue last night and slap the drinks out of my hand?"

She chuckled as she hugged him. "Because, my friend, you were having fun."

"Please tell me I didn't hula dance."

"Oh yeah, you did." Gia chuckled as she took a sip of her coffee.

"Was I any good?"

"You were so amazing that two guys came over and stuffed money in your pocket," Lindsey said as she scooted off the barstool and headed to the refrigerator. A flash of warmth came over her as her eyes meet Gia's.

"Are you bullshitting me?" He reached in his front pockets and pulled out two five-dollar bills. "Damn, I must have been really good." He let the bills fall onto the counter, then glanced at them. "Where are you two beauties off to today?"

"I'm taking Gia to Crenshaw Caverns," Lindsey said as she broke eye contact and topped off her coffee with more soymilk.

"Thought they were closed on Wednesdays," Paul said as he returned to rubbing his temples.

"They are. Paiton said she would open it up for us so Gia could have a private tour."

"Paiton the pit bull?" Paul said with surprise. "Damn, girl, you got some pull. It'd be easier to get a favor from God. How'd you make that happen?"

"I may have mentioned the *L Online* angle, and she may have mentioned back how awesome it would be if her photo made it into the article." Lindsey's real motive was to create another memory that meant something. The caverns were one of the places she'd go to decompress while Jenn or Paul sat with her mom. The untouched beauty of the cave not only calmed her, it brought her to a place of balance. Today, she was hoping the experience would bring her and Gia closer together.

"You bribed her?" Paul said in a soft voice as he slowly brought his cup to his lips.

"I wouldn't call it bribery. More like an exchange of mutual understanding." Lindsey smiled.

Paul laughed. "Ow." He placed his cup back on the counter and returned to rubbing his head. "That hurt."

Gia pulled a small bottle of aspirin from her purse. "You might want to take two of these."

He glanced up. "Thank you."

Lindsey leaned in and kissed him on the cheek. "You going to be okay for a while?"

He shooed them away. "Go. Enjoy. I'll be fine. By the time we head over to Jenn's this afternoon, I'll be good as new."

As they hopped in the van, the butterflies in Lindsey's stomach took flight. Sitting next to Gia reinvigorated last night's sexual energy. She had tingles in parts of her body she didn't think were even capable of having that type of sensation. She tightened her grip on the steering wheel and tipped her head from side to side to relieve some of the tension settling in her shoulders. Should she bring up the *almost* kiss that *almost* happened? Or should she wait to see if Gia took the lead? She let out a long exhale. She was petrified that Gia no longer felt the same way this morning. After all, they had a few drinks last night, and the alcohol could have played a role. On the other hand, she had felt a vibe between them since the river. There was definitely a mutual attraction. *Oh my God, just ask her already before the butterflies explode.* "Gia, um, I was wondering…"

Gia was staring out the open window. "Hmm?" she said without turning.

"I, um…" She stumbled and decided to drop the question for now. Gia seemed to be lost in a thought that probably had nothing to do with last night. "It's nice out, isn't it?"

"I don't think I have felt this relaxed in a long time," Gia said as she turned. "And I don't think I'll ever get tired of the green. It's really beautiful."

"Well, you might think twice about that view come winter. Things can get pretty depressing and dreary around here. The gray skies and bare trees can turn you a bit melancholy."

"I can't even imagine. I love the winter. It's Phoenix's best time of the year."

Lindsey thought back to the pictures of San Louis Obispo during the winter holidays: people smiling and looking like they were having a blast hanging out on the sunny beach with Santa hats and T-shirts on. *That* was going to be her. She was going to be one of those people on that beach, having a life of snowless winters, sunshine, and sporting a golden tan.

Stop, Lindsey scolded herself, stop living life in reverse. She could replay all the shouda, coulda, wouldas, and it still wasn't going to change the outcome. The job and the opportunity were long gone. She'd made the right decision by staying, and it was time she stopped looking at it as though she was a victim of circumstance. Her dad's death, turning down the opportunity to move, her mom's Alzheimer's…those were not unfortunate things that *happened to her*. No, those things might have fallen in her lap, but they most certainly didn't *happen* to her.

"What are you thinking?" Gia asked.

"Oh, I was just thinking about…" She trailed off as she glanced at Gia. If someone had told her last month that she would be sitting across from her all-time favorite online crush, she would have thought they were crazy. And yet, here she was. Maybe some of the things that had *happened* in her life were just detours to unexpected destinations. "I was just wondering what it would have been like if I had taken that job in California."

"You probably would have loved it. California is awesome. I used to go there a lot, hang out with friends in LA and then drive up the coast. But like every other place, it definitely has its share of shit, and the earthquakes can be a bit unnerving. But it really is beautiful out there."

Lindsey groaned. "I wouldn't know. I've never been out of Missouri."

"Shut the fuck up. Are you serious?"

Lindsey frowned. Since her mother's death, she'd finally had the freedom she'd so desperately craved but was at a loss as to what to do with it. The idea of a quest seemed more appealing when it was an out-of-reach dream. "Totally serious."

"Well, I don't want to tell you how to live your life, but my advice is, get out of your Missouri bubble. There are so many amazing things to see and do out there."

Lindsey smiled. "Says the woman who has been holed up in her house for the last five years."

Gia seemed to turn somber and looked away.

"I'm sorry, Gia, I didn't mean—"

"No," she said more to the wind than Lindsey. "You're right. I've felt so sorry for myself all these years that I forgot about life outside of my own little bubble."

Lindsey nodded as she focused on the road and wondered if that was what she'd been doing all these years as well. Growing up, she'd pouted her way through a lot of her childhood because her family never had enough money to afford all the things she wanted. After Jasmine broke up with her, she definitely cried a river, and caregiving for her mom came with many moments of *why me*.

They traveled the remaining twenty minutes in silence until she pulled off the freeway. "Crenshaw's isn't a very big cave, but it's one of the little gems in this area." Lindsey hoped her play on words would make Gia smile, and it did.

She pulled into the empty lot in front of the entrance. Paiton waved as she strolled up to them. "Hey, Paiton," Lindsey said as she hopped out.

"Linds." Paiton focused on Gia. "And who's this beautiful woman?" She extended her hand as soon as Gia opened her door. "Please, let me help you out."

"Gia, Paiton. Paiton, Gia." Lindsey introduced them as Gia accepted Paiton's hand.

"Is that." Lindsey squinted at Paiton's face. "Are you wearing…"

Paiton stiffened and shot her a look that conveyed that she would be skating on thin ice if she completed that sentence.

Lindsey dropped the subject. In the twenty years that she had known Paiton, she had never once seen her wear any form of makeup. Although Paton only dated feminine women, she once told Lindsey that she had never had a desire in dressing or looking "like that."

"It's very nice to meet you," Gia said as she pulled her hand free.

"Welcome to Crenshaw Caverns, I'll be your personal tour guide for the day. But I thought, before we get started, you could get a picture of our sign." Paiton hustled over to the wooden Crenshaw Caverns sign, struck a pose, and held a smile as Gia dug in her purse for her phone.

"Yep, that would be perfect," Gia said as she snapped a couple of shots of Paiton, then gave her a thumbs-up.

Lindsey rolled her eyes. Paiton was coming on strong right out of the gate, and she was equal parts amused and jealous. As Paiton placed a hand on Gia's shoulder and escorted her to the entrance, she started to wonder if bringing her here was a mistake.

Paiton opened up the lobby, grabbed her jacket, and escorted them over to an elevator. "You can place your purse and all personal items in one of these lockers. Once we get down to the cave, our first stop will be in a decontamination station, where I'll spray down your shoes with rubbing alcohol to kill any fungus or contaminants that may be on them. There will be no binoculars, flashlights, or photography except for the areas designated for photo taking. No food, gum, tobacco products, or drinks. There will be no touching or damaging the formations, littering or tossing coins. Any questions?"

Lindsey and Gia shook their heads.

Paiton leaned over and softly said to Gia, "Now would be a good time to put your jacket on. The cave is always around sixty-eight degrees. Linds told me you were from Phoenix, so that might feel a bit chilly to you."

Gia shrugged into her jacket and smiled. "Thank you."

Paiton nodded and summoned the elevator. A few seconds later, they entered the underground world of huge stalactites and stalagmites lit with multicolored lights.

"Wow," Gia said in a low voice as she turned in a circle.

"How are you feeling?" Lindsey whispered. Gia had shared that she had never been in a cave because she thought being hundreds of feet underground would make her feel claustrophobic. But Lindsey had reassured her that Crenshaw Caverns had a spacious and open feel, and she thought they would be just fine.

"It's so beautiful," she said as she zipped up her jacket.

"I take it that you're okay?" Lindsey focused on Gia's childlike expression. This was exactly what she had hoped for when she'd decided to bring Gia here. She'd wanted to create a wonderful memory—that she would be a part of—when Gia looked back on this moment.

"I'm fine. It's nothing like I envisioned. It's amazing," Gia mumbled as she continued to spin.

"I'm glad you like it."

Paiton's hand came down between them and landed on Gia's shoulder. "Why don't you walk next to me so I can give you the full history of the cave, its formations, and all its occupants?"

"Occupants?" Gia said with worry in her voice. "You mean like bats?"

"Bats and other small critters. But don't you worry." Paiton stepped close. "You're safe with me." She guided Gia forward down a narrow-paved path framed with banisters and dimly lit ground lights.

Lindsey glared as Paiton whisked Gia away. What the fuck? She wanted to slap Paiton's hand off Gia's shoulder, but at the same time, who was she to Gia? True, they seemed to be connecting, and they had almost kissed last night, but Lindsey was also painfully aware that in a few days, Gia would be back in Phoenix, and she would still be…what? What would she be? Single, pathetic, and stuck in Missouri.

She shoved her hands in her front pockets and grumbled to herself as she shuffled behind them. "Missouri isn't holding you back, you are," she whispered to herself. Maybe it was finally time for her to book that long awaited trip to California and stop waiting for that certain someone to come into her life, swoop her up, and rescue her. It was time she rescued herself.

As they wandered through the cave, stopping to look at the beauty of nature's masterpiece, Lindsey started making travel plans for the first time since college. She could use the money she had earmarked for the new kitchen countertop. She's lived with the gashes, stains, and scratches in the laminate this long, what was another year or two? By the time they took a seat to marvel at the section of the cave that Paiton called the great room, she had made a promise to herself. After Gia returned to Phoenix, Lindsey was going to book herself a flight to California. And who knew, she might even stay.

"Take a seat, you two." Paiton pointed to the five rows of cement bench seats. "What we have before us is a room that is four hundred feet long and two hundred and forty feet wide, full of stalagmites and stalactites. Trivia fact, the force of gravity limits the buildup of the stalactites." Paiton focused on Gia as she hiked her pants and winked. "Crenshaw is considered a living cave, as it's constantly changing and growing. Now, settle in while I go hit the lights." Paiton shuffled over to a switch hidden behind a rock.

"What do you think so far?" Lindsey scooted up against Gia. She knew what was coming next, and she wanted to be right next to her when it happened.

"I think—"

"I'm going to shut the path lights off for a moment before I turn the spotlights on," Paiton announced. "While in darkness, take a moment to listen to the cave." The cave went completely dark. It was the true definition of pitch-black, and outside of a slow drip in the distance, it was also the definition of absolute silence. Lindsey gently placed a hand on Gia's thigh and squeezed. Her stomach bottomed out as she shivered. Although the touch was subtle, the reaction in her body was explosive.

"And now the lights," Paiton said in a voice that was almost a whisper.

A flip of a switch later and multicolored spotlights lit up a large chamber that seemed to have no end. Stalagmites, ridged and scalloped, rose from the floor, and crystalline shields protruding from the walls took on the color of the lights as a rainbow of colors played out in front of them.

Gia gasped as she placed a hand over Lindsey's, sending a cascade of goose bumps tingling down her body. She slowly turned her hand up and gently stroked Gia's palm. The touch was so erotic that she found herself being pulled closer. The urge to kiss her was overwhelming. Even if it was only a soft touch to her cheek, she wanted to somehow mark this moment. She licked her lips and leaned in.

"Pretty awesome, huh?" Paiton sat next to Gia, causing her to jump and their hands to separate. "When I tell people the dimensions, they don't totally understand how big it really is. To put that in perspective, it's larger than a football field."

"It's so…" Gia trailed off.

"Beautiful." Paiton filled in the word as she stared at Gia.

Are you fucking serious? Lindsey felt like reaching around Gia's back and slapping Paiton's face. Could she be any more obnoxiously intrusive? Lindsey clasped her hands together as she dug her thumb in her palm and began rubbing the frustration away.

Paiton took off her jacket and draped it around Gia. "You looked a little chilled when I sat down."

Gia shrugged off the jacket and handed it back. "Actually. I'm fine, but thank you anyway."

Lindsey smiled as she glanced at Gia, who winked at her. The gesture was not only received, it sent a flash of heat through her body. Gia had let her know where she stood. And as petty as it seemed, Lindsey felt like standing and mimicking an excited football player who'd just scored a touchdown. *Take that, Paiton.* But instead, she took a breath, grinned, and turned to take in the great room. Although she had seen it multiple times, right now, it looked more spectacular than ever.

They sat in silence. There was no need for conversation as they enjoyed the view that nature had kept secret for millions of years. Finally, Paiton stood and said they needed to get going.

"But before we go," Paiton said. "You might want to snap a few photos. Want me to stand in the shot?" she threw out as she walked to the edge and leaned against the handrail.

"Um, yeah. Sure. That'd be great." Gia took several pictures.

Paiton grinned. "Those will probably make good ones for your article. And there's a place just up ahead that you can take some more. In fact, you should be in them with me."

Gia nodded. "Um, okay."

Lindsey rolled her eyes and placed her hands on her face as she counted to ten. She had never had the urge to push someone over a cliff until right now, and she chuckled at the disconcerting thought. Paiton was definitely pinging her jealousy nerves. And it had been a long time since those were pulled.

"All right, follow me." Paiton shouldered next to Gia as she led them through the remaining parts of the cave. Forty-five minutes later, they were standing in front of the minivan, thanking Paiton for the tour.

"It was very nice to meet you, Gia, and here." Paiton shoved a brochure toward her. "If you need more facts for your article. And I, um, I also took the liberty of writing my cell number on it. You know, in case you have any questions, or just want to—"

"Thanks again, Paiton." Lindsey cut her off. "But we gotta hit the road."

Paiton lunged and grabbed the passenger door handle. "Here, let me get that for you."

Gia smiled. "Thanks, Paiton. The tour was truly spectacular." She hopped into her seat.

"I'll be at Masquerades later tonight. Maybe I'll see you there and you know, buy you a drink or something?"

Lindsey started the ignition. "Not tonight, Paiton. We have other plans, but thanks again."

"Oh, okay. Well, then, maybe another night? Anyway, you have my number," Paiton said as she closed Gia's door, stepped back, and waved.

Gia lowered the window as Lindsey headed for the freeway. "Thank you again," she called.

"I'm so sorry about that," Lindsey said. She knew Paiton could be overbearing, but she had never seen her be so pushy. She cocked her head. Or maybe Paiton really wasn't being as pushy as she thought. Maybe Lindsey was just feeling protective of her newfound feelings.

"About what?" Gia asked.

Lindsey snorted. "You're honestly going to sit there and tell me you were clueless about what Paiton was doing?"

Gia laughed. "Oh, that. Well, don't worry about me. Although I may be rusty, I can handle myself. And just in case you're wondering, I'm not interested in her."

Lindsey's butterflies responded to the news. Her hands became a little sweaty, and she thought the look in Gia's eyes created a perfect segue to talk about last night. "Really? So, um, I was wondering if we could talk about last—"

The ringing of Gia's phone interrupted her. "Hold that thought. This is probably Stacy letting me know she landed." Lindsey saw the smile slowly fade from Gia's face when she looked at the screen and hit the speaker button. "Hi, Mom. Is everything okay?"

"Guess what we are now?"

"Um, I'm not quite sure I understand the question."

"Fish hobbyist." Her mom's voice held a tone of disgust. "Because, apparently, while I was at the store last week, your father opened the door to a guy selling koi pond construction and he just up and whipped out his credit card and bought the deluxe one. It's got a rock waterfall and everything."

Gia let out a long sigh. "Give me the name of the company, and I'll give them a call."

"Too late, they're here digging up the backyard now."

"Put dad on the phone."

"Can't. He locked himself in the back bedroom because I took the credit card out of his wallet and cut it up. But hold on and I'll let him know you want to talk to him."

"No, that's—"

"Henry!" The yell was so screeching, it startled Lindsey, and she jerked the wheel to the right. "Your daughter wants to talk to you."

"Sorry." Lindsey mouthed as she corrected the wheel and concentrated on the road.

"He said he doesn't want to talk, and maybe that's a good thing because he isn't in the best of moods right now."

"Well, Mom, looks like you got yourself a koi pond. You've always said you wanted a fountain in the backyard. Now you have a waterfall. Maybe you'll enjoy it once it's up and running."

"Don't you be taking your father's side on this," she scolded.

"I'm not," Gia said. "I'm just saying…look, I'm kinda in the middle of something right now, can I call you later?"

"Of course you can, dear, I'm still just so tickled pink you're out and…oh no, you don't," her mom yelled. "Not so close to my rose bush. Young man, don't you even think about digging up—"

The line went dead. Gia sat in silence for a moment, then turned to Lindsey. "I'm so sorry about that."

Lindsey felt a pang of emotion. What she wouldn't give to still be able to talk to her mom. Just to hear her voice again and tell her how much she loved her would be priceless. "No worries. Your mom sounds like a character."

"That's putting it mildly." Gia tossed her phone back in her purse.

"A koi pond, huh?" She could tell by Gia's bewildered expression that now was not the time to bring up last night.

"I guess so."

They both laughed. Everything inside Lindsey wanted to reach over and entwine her fingers with hers. Gia, who had seemed to be such a disappointment, such a trigger to the pain of her past, was turning out to be one of the best things that had ever happened to her. As Gia started in on story after story of her parents' mishaps, Lindsey couldn't help but smile. One of the things she missed about a relationship was knowing all the important players in the other person's life and sharing in their stories. Listening to Gia gave her the sense that she was sharing more than just time with her right now…she was sharing an intimate part of her life. And that alone made Lindsey want to be with her all the more.

❖

Gia bolted out of the house and hurried down the walk as Stacy jumped out of her car and raised her arms. "Hold the presses, and someone get me a drink. Stacy's here!"

"Am I glad to see you." Gia wrapped her arms around Stacy in a warm embrace. Although she no longer felt the need to be rescued, having Stacy by her side would not only provide an extra layer of comfort, she couldn't wait to tell her about Lindsey. Their conversations had been almost nonexistent lately as Stacy put in long days at work and equally long nights with women.

When they broke the hug, Stacy gave Gia the once-over. "Okay, wow, you're outside like a functioning adult, you're not melting, and you look great. This is either sorcery or you and I need to do some serious catching up."

"We definitely need to do some…" Gia paused as Paul approached. "Paul, this is my best friend, Stacy. Stacy, Paul," Gia proudly introduced.

Paul leaned in and kissed Stacy's cheeks. "Are all the women in Phoenix as beautiful as you two?"

"Paul, you're my new best friend." Stacy hooked her arm around his. "Now take me to my room so I can freshen up for this party Gia's told me about."

"Let me get your bag." He turned toward Stacy's luggage.

Gia lunged for it. "I got it." She waved him off. Her suitcase still had a large dent in it, and she didn't want Stacy's expensive carry-on to suffer the same fate.

"You sure?" he called over his shoulder. "Because it's a service we provide."

"Yeah, no worries, I got it." Gia wheeled the luggage behind her. She watched the two of them fall into what looked like a comfortable conversation, as though they were old souls reacquainted. And there was something about that that warmed her heart. And for the first time since she'd arrived, she grew sad at the thought of leaving. There was a lot about this place she was going to miss. Especially Lindsey.

Paul escorted Stacy to the room next to Gia's. "Here you go."

"Wow," Stacy said as she spun in a circle. "Who decorated this room?"

"I did." Paul smiled.

"If you lived in Phoenix, I could get you some work. This room is stunning."

"If you think the room blows you away, wait until you taste his cooking," Gia added as the smell of freshly baked pies was causing her stomach to grumble.

"If it tastes anywhere close to the way it smells, you'll find this mama camped out in the kitchen grazing for the next few days." Stacy smiled.

"He also has a descent wine collection."

Stacy put her hand to her heart. "Mercy me, I do believe I'm never leaving this fine establishment."

"Meet me in the kitchen later tonight, and I'll hook you up." Paul walked to the door and turned. "As soon as she's settled in, we'll head over to Jenn's. I'll be down in the main room hanging out until then."

"Thanks," Gia called after him.

"This place is so charming." Stacy hoisted her luggage onto the bed and unzipped the sides. "Well." She grabbed a pair of khaki capris and a peach-colored shirt. "How's it going with Lindsey?" She cocked her head as though scrutinizing her combination choice.

Gia paused. The question wasn't so much how was Lindsey, the question was more like, how was Gia now that she had woken up? She turned and smiled. "She's uh…we're um…"

"Shut the fuck up. You're into her." Stacy waved a finger at Gia as she grinned.

"I have to admit, Lindsey isn't at all what I expected. She's really nice and super cute and easy to talk to and…we almost kissed on the porch last night." Gia grinned. She was falling in love, and even though there was still a part of her that resisted that reality, the rest of her was wholeheartedly embracing it.

Stacy let out a loud squeal as she grabbed Gia and suffocated her in a bear hug.

Paul burst into the room holding a broom over his shoulder like he was about to swing a baseball bat. "I heard someone scream. What happened? Is it that mouse again?"

Stacy broke the hug. "Someone here is in love." Stacy patted Gia on the shoulders.

"Wait a second." Paul huffed, still white-knuckling the broom handle. "I just need to be perfectly clear. There's no mouse, bat, other rodent, big hairy spider, or bug in here?"

Stacy scrunched her nose. "I should hope not."

He let the broom fall from his shoulders. "Okay, phew. Because normally when that happens, Jeff is the one who comes to the rescue. This whole role reversal thing I've had to do since he's be in Oklahoma is stressing me out."

Stacy wrapped him in a warm embrace. "Coming up here with broom in hand, ready to protect two damsels in distress, makes you our hero."

"Make that three in distress because holy shit, I need a drink after that. You about scared the shit out of me." He walked out, trailing the broom behind him. "I'll be in the kitchen downing a bottle of wine and calming my nerves."

Gia giggled. "We'll be right down, and thank you again for being our hero."

"My superpowers lie in the kitchen," he called out. "Next time you squeal, do it over one of my sticky buns."

"He makes homemade cinnamon rolls?" Stacy cocked her head.

Gia nodded. "Every morning and they're the best you've ever had."

"If I'm not in my room tomorrow morning, you'll know where to find me. Now then, back to you and your libido. I'm really happy for you, Gia. It's nice to see you normal again."

"Okay, first of all, thanks. I think. And second, I'm going to overlook the reference that comment makes on my past character." Gia frowned. She had identified with far worse. In fact, she'd had moments where she was so sick of herself and the situation that she'd created that she had cussed herself out and verbally beaten herself down. Which only perpetuated her isolated state.

"When do I get to meet Lindsey?" Stacy asked.

"She'll be at Jenn's party."

"Tell me about this Jenn." Stacy grabbed a sundress and threw the other clothes into a dresser drawer.

"You'll love her. She's just like you." Gia grinned as she mentally compared the two.

"Single? Attractive? Up for a good time?" Stacy smirked.

Gia nodded. "Like I said, she's just like you."

Stacy cocked her head. "Interesting," she said in a soft voice as she shooed Gia out of her room. "Okay, now off you go while I shower and get freshened up."

"I'll be downstairs talking to Paul."

Almost an hour later, Stacy sauntered into the kitchen. She had a tasteful amount of makeup on, a peach cotton sundress, and over-sized brown sunglasses. If it was Hollywood instead of Jacobe, she'd fit right in. Here, she'd definitely stand out.

"I was starting to worry about what you were doing up there," Gia said.

"Refreshing this body takes time. Which I'm happy to report, is now completely renewed and ready to go."

Paul rounded the kitchen island. "I love your makeup."

"And I love a man with impeccable taste." Stacy smiled.

"So do I. Now grab those pies and let's go make an entrance."

They grabbed the food and shuffled out of the house. Jenn lived in a small redbrick home with a well-manicured yard. A typical Jacobe house, from what Gia had noticed. They headed to the backyard. A group of people mingled with drinks in hand, a dozen more were in the pool, and another handful were standing in line waiting to get their haircut at a makeshift station in the corner.

"Who is that gorgeous woman cutting hair?" Stacy said as she lowered her sunglasses.

"That's Jenn, and according to Paul, she's the best stylist in town."

"Paul, Gia," Lindsey called as she jogged over.

"Wow. I love your hair," Gia said. The haircut was a shorter version of her normal style, but it seemed to frame her face in a way that made her eyes bigger and her lips more kissable. Or maybe it wasn't the hairstyle so as much as the welcoming smile.

"I was one of Jenn's first Guinea pigs." Lindsey lightly touched her hair. "Everyone who wants a haircut today gets one for the price of a donation. Any amount is accepted, and all the money goes to the Jacobe animal shelter."

"It's, uh…" Gia stumbled. "It's a really a great cut." There was something about her that seemed different. Sure, the new cut and style made her absolutely adorable, but there was something else. Something beyond the physical. Or was she sensing it from herself? Now that she had confessed her feelings, did that make them real? As though airing them out seemed to not only validate them but also intensify them.

Stacy broke the trance "I'm Stacy, the other person standing here that Gia has suddenly forgotten about."

"Oh, um, sorry, so sorry. Stacy, this is Lindsey." Gia beamed.

"Nice to meet you." Lindsey shook her hand.

"It is a pleasure to meet you. Where would you like us to put these?" Stacy displayed the pie.

Lindsey glanced around. "Let's put 'em on that table."

They followed her to a banquet-sized foldout table that had a variety of pastries, finger sandwiches, chips, and dips scattered on top. An assortment of beverages sat in coolers underneath.

Stacy pulled out a bottle and held it out to Gia. "Beer?"

"Yes, thanks." The humidity was hovering around the sweltering level, and she needed something to cool her body and calm her nerves. She wanted to be alone with Lindsey and away from the crowd.

"Lindsey? Paul?" Stacy asked "Beer?"

Lindsey nodded as Paul shook his head. "After what happened last night, I think it's safer if I stick to soda."

"You owe me a story." Stacy smiled at him. "Now then." She handed over a beer and a can of soda. "Let's go mark our territory and partake in one of life's many fascinations: people watching."

"I'm right there with you." He clinked his can on her bottle.

An hour later, Jenn shuffled over to where they were sitting. "You guys are the last on my…" She trialed off as she turned to Stacy. "Well. Hello." Jenn smiled as she leaned down and extended her hand. "I'm Jenn, you up for a cut?"

"I'm Stacy, and I thought you'd never ask. Hold my beer, Gia." But Stacy released the bottle before she had a chance to grab it, and it fell to the ground, spilling on the grass.

"Wow, correct me if I'm wrong, but I'm sensing chemistry between those two," Lindsey said.

Gia wanted to tell her that Stacy pretty much had chemistry with any woman with a pulse, but there was something in Stacy's vibe toward Jenn that made her wonder. "Yeah, I think you might be right," she mumbled as Stacy tilted her head back in animated laughter. "Um." Gia refocused on Lindsey. "Are most of these people friends of yours?" She gestured to a group playing in the pool.

"Most are casual acquaintances and a handful work for Jenn. Jacobe is small enough that sooner or later, you've either met everyone in the gay community, or you've heard about them. Huh, Paul?"

"You got that right. Uh-oh," he said in a soft voice. "Pit bull at twelve o'clock."

Paiton came strolling up to them. "Well, well."

Lindsey groaned. "Paiton, wow. I didn't realize you'd be here."

"The grapevine, what can I say? When I heard Jenn was having a backyard barbeque, I figured I'd find you guys here."

Paiton extended her hand to Gia. "Come with me so I can introduce you to everyone since Linds and Paul seem to be keeping you all to themselves."

Gia glanced over at Lindsey, then back to Paiton. "No, that's okay. I…"

"Come on, I won't keep you to myself for long, I promise." Paiton winked.

Gia swallowed hard as she waited for Lindsey to come to her rescue. Not that she couldn't take care of herself—she could—but right now, she was still feeling a little overwhelmed in the presence of so many strangers, and her security blanket was busy getting her hair cut and flirting with Jenn.

"You know what?" Lindsey chimed in. "We're actually doing fine just chilling out here. Besides, she's with me."

The excitement those three words created in Gia's stomach took her breath away. Was that true? Was she with Lindsey, or was she just saying that to get rid of Paiton?

"Is that right?" Paiton huffed as she retrieved her hand, hiked up her shorts, and glanced at Gia. "I'll be over by the pool in case you get bored with your present company. Just sayin'." Paiton glared at Lindsey and walked away.

"Ya know," Paul said. "There's just something about Paiton that makes me want to puke."

Lindsey snarled. "It's called her personality. I should have told her to go fuck herself."

He crunched his face. "I've always wondered about that statement. If you think about it, it kinda takes the charm out of masturbation."

They laughed as Lindsey's words echoed in Gia's head. *She's with me.* She wanted to lean over and ask if Lindsey had really meant that. Because if she had, Gia would be honored to be by her side. She leaned in. "Um, about what you said to Paiton."

"Okay, everyone," Stacy said loudly as she and Jenn walked up. "What do you think?" Stacy fluffed her new shoulder-length style and grinned.

"Wow, Stace, you really look great," Gia said with a smile.

"Your turn, Gia," Jenn said.

"Oh no." Gia shyly rubbed a hand down her long hair. "I'm good. Maybe you could do Paul instead?"

"I cut his hair last week. Now come on, you're my last of the day, and I really want a beer, so off we go." She extended her hand.

"Oh, well um…" She trailed off as everyone was gesturing in encouragement. "Maybe just a trim," she said as she took Jenn's hand and followed her to the station.

Jenn patted the back of her salon chair. "Okay, you, take a seat." She placed the vinyl cape around Gia's neck. "What would you like?"

"Just a trim." Gia held her finger and thumb a few centimeters apart for reference.

"Hmm." Jenn cocked her head as she ran her fingers through Gia's hair. "Sure you don't want a little more? I could take several inches off the back, layer it, and sexy you up a bit."

Gia was about to protest that, no, she didn't need *sexying up*. Or a fashionable layered look. Her hair was fine just the way it was. But as she glanced over her shoulder at Lindsey sitting there looking cute as hell, she decided that maybe she could go for a little spicing up. "Yeah, okay. Sexy me up a bit. It's been way too long." One more thing from her past that she needed to shed.

When she'd been with Audrey, she had always wanted to cut her hair short, but Audrey had protested that women with short hair looked too butch for her taste. Because of that, Gia had continued to conform to the person Audrey had wanted her to be. The hair, the clothes, and their friends. Her life had nothing to do with herself. She had just been an extension of Audrey.

"Attagirl." Jenn pushed down on the hydraulic pump that raised the chair. "Now just relax and let me do my thing."

Gia closed her eyes at the feel of cool mist on her head. She silently whispered a fuck you to Audrey and her controlling ways as she let Jenn dance around her. Each stand of hair that fell took part of her past with it. Maybe it really was time to sexy up a bit. Hell, when was the last time she'd honestly felt sexy at all? A lifetime ago. She snorted. A lifetime of feeling trapped in a dead-end relationship and feeling frozen in a state of depression and anxiety. *Well, to hell with that.* Whatever Jenn envisioned for her, even if it made her feel uncomfortable, she was going to embrace it. New beginnings. She smiled.

"My work here is done," Jenn announced as she massaged a palmful of gel into Gia's scalp. She stepped back, nodded, and handed her a mirror. "I think this look suits you much better."

Gia took a breath as she held the mirror up and stared at a shorter, layered hairstyle. Her first thought was that she looked younger, but upon further inspection, she decided that, no, it wasn't that she looked younger, it was more like she looked… what? *Lighter* was the word she finally settled on. For the past several years, the face that had stared back in the mirror had always seemed so miserable and dreary. The face staring at her now was anything but. "I love it." She smiled as she handed the mirror back. "Thank you."

Jenn spun the chair around so Gia could see Lindsey smiling as she walked toward them. "I think someone else also approves."

Gia stood and exhaled. Lindsey's eyes sparkled in the late afternoon sun, and each step caused her pulse to quicken.

"You look beautiful," Lindsey said as she reached to Gia's face and gently tucked a strand of hair behind her ear.

Beautiful? When was the last time someone had called her beautiful? She couldn't remember, and that reality caused sadness to wash over her. She placed a hand over Lindsey's and shivered. How could the innocent act of touching hands be such an absolute turn-on?

"Are you cold?" Lindsey asked.

Gia squeezed her hand. "It wasn't that kind of shiver." She leaned into Lindsey as they walked back to the group.

Paul whistled. "Wow. You look stunning."

"Thanks." She shyly smiled, then glanced to Stacy for approval.

Stacy nodded and gave her a thumbs-up. "You look fantastic," she mouthed.

Gia rubbed her hand over the back of her bare neck. Why hadn't she cut her hair after she and Audrey had broken up? She had always wanted to, but there was still that damn voice in the back of her head nagging her about her looks and what she should and shouldn't do. It was nice to finally have that voice silenced.

As the sun drifted across the sky and the afternoon turned to evening, the crowd thinned, and by nightfall, it was just the five of them. Gia had suggested they call out for pizza an hour ago, and now Gia sat content with her legs dangling in Jenn's pool, enjoying the pleasant evening breeze.

Paul rubbed his stomach. "I have a food baby in my belly."

Jenn gently patted his stomach as if playing the bongos. Paul laughed, then bent forward. "Okay, okay, stop. It hurts when I laugh." He slapped at Jenn's hands. "All right, you two." He pointed. "Time to head out. I'm getting tired."

"I'll take them home." Lindsey said. "I mean, if that's okay?"

Gia and Stacy nodded and mumbled their agreement.

"Okay, then, me and my baby bump are out of here, see you guys later." Paul stood.

"Don't wait up," Gia called. She was enjoying being with Lindsey, and she didn't want it to end anytime soon.

"Hadn't planned to." He waved as he shuffled out of the yard.

"He's okay to drive, right?" Jenn slurred a bit.

Lindsey nodded. "He's fine. Unlike us, he's been drinking soda all day."

"Smart boy." Jenn said, then leaned over and whispered something in Stacy's ear.

Stacy stood and stumbled a bit as she grabbed Jenn's hand. "Jenn's going to give me a tour of her house. You guys going to be okay out here for a while?" Stacy said as she followed Jenn and staggered up the porch steps.

"Yep, we're good," Lindsey called. "I think they're a little drunk."

"Oh, and we're not?" Gia snorted as she leaned back on her elbows and stared at the night sky. The air was still, and the stars twinkled and danced above her in a silent display of beauty. "The sky is so…" She turned to Lindsey and sat in stunned disbelief. Lindsey was standing at the side of the pool, stripping off her clothes. "What…" Gia cleared her throat.

"What are you doing?" Holy shit. Her brain struggled to sober up so she could enjoy the scenery.

Lindsey winked as she kicked off the last article of clothing and dove into the pool. "Come on in, the water feels wonderful." She backstroked away.

Gia jumped up and wiggled out of her clothes as fast as she could. Her legs had been dangling in the water for the past hour, so she knew the pool was nice and warm. She wasted no time diving in. "Feels nice," she said as she came up for air and swam to the steps. She settled on the bottom one, making sure her upper body was still fully submerged. She paused for a moment as she gazed at Lindsey. Whether she wanted to admit it or not, the past several days had changed her, had made her want things she'd thought she could do without. And right now, the desire to be touched was the thing she wanted the most.

"Yeah. Jenn hates to swim in chilly water, so she keeps the heater cranked all summer." Lindsey pushed off and swam over. "You look a little nervous. Don't tell me you've never skinny-dipped before?"

"It's not that. In Phoenix, we have tall brick walls that separate the houses and allow for privacy. Here, there's nothing," she said as she shyly glanced around.

"Well." Lindsey stood in the shallow water and slowly sauntered over. "You don't need to worry about that. Jenn bought this place because the closest neighbor is over an acre away."

The water ran down Lindsey's face and over her beautiful, perky breasts. Breasts that held Gia in a trance as they came closer. Lindsey stopped within inches and motioned for Gia to stand. "I want to see you." She softly beckoned.

Lindsey was so close when Gia stood that their nipples met. Their lips were only millimeters apart. "You're so beautiful," Gia whispered. Her lips brushed ever so gently against Lindsey's with each word.

Lindsey placed her hands behind Gia's head, rubbed her fingers through her hair, and leaned in and kissed her in a way that released something raw. In that moment, she wanted Lindsey to go deep inside her and scratch the itch that had been building, an ache so primal, it was making the simple task of speech impossible to achieve beyond grunts and groans. Maybe it was the sensation of finally reemerging from her cocoon. Or the love she was beginning to feel. Or maybe it was nothing more than a night of letting loose with a beautiful woman. Whatever it was, she embraced the intense feelings and returned Lindsey's kiss with equal parts passion and desire.

Lindsey finally broke the kiss as she cupped Gia's breast and started sucking her nipples. They were half-submerged, and she could feel Lindsey's tongue and the water swirl around them, exciting her more and more. "I want…" She moaned.

Lindsey moved her face close to Gia's ear. "Talk to me," she whispered as she pressed her body firmly against Gia's and tickled her neck with her tongue.

"I…uh." Gia groaned as she tried to catch her breath. She backed Lindsey against the side of the pool, leaned in, and pressed into her as she kissed her long and hard. When they parted, she said, "On the ledge."

"What?" Lindsey whispered through a heavy breath.

"The ledge," Gia said. "I want you to sit on the edge of the pool."

Lindsey looked behind her and nodded. Gia helped her and took a moment to cup warm water in her hands to gently drizzle over Lindsey's thighs.

"Are you cold?" she asked.

"No," Lindsey said in a barely audible voice as she scooted even closer to the edge and leaned back on her arms.

Gia gently spread Lindsey's legs and licked the length of her thigh to her clitoris. She paused, letting her tongue tickle and tease before traveling down Lindsey's other thigh.

"Tease," Lindsey said through heavy breaths as she arched her back.

"Not for long," Gia whispered through thigh kisses. "I promise."

Again, Gia cupped a handful of water and poured it over Lindsey's lower body, letting the last of it drip between Lindsey's legs. When the last drop fell, she lowered her hand until the tips of her fingers touched Lindsey's wetness. The tightening of her thighs told Gia she was ready to receive what she was about to offer. She slowly bent and let her tongue become one with her fingers.

"Yes," Lindsey whispered as Gia began kissing and licking around Lindsey's wetness. "Yes."

A shiver shot up Gia at the understanding of what that one word conveyed, the permission it granted, and she gladly fulfilled Lindsey's request. She slowly licked Lindsey up and down, and the taste of chlorine mixed with her wetness. Lindsey pulled her legs out of the water and wrapped them around Gia's shoulders, pressing her clit deeper into Gia's mouth. She moaned loud and long, and Gia could feel her thigh muscles tightening. A deeper, throatier sound told her that Lindsey was ready for more. She licked and sucked harder, and the moment she sensed Lindsey coming, she entered her with two fingers and stroked her fast and deep.

Seconds later, Lindsey cried out, hunched forward, and held the back of Gia's head. Gia could feel Lindsey's orgasm continue to pulse as she maintained pressure on her clit. After a beat, Lindsey relaxed and let out a long breath. She took a step back and let Lindsey slide off the ledge and into the water.

"I hope I didn't suffocate you at the end there," Lindsey whispered through a heavy breath.

"On the contrary." Gia leaned in and kissed her. "I totally got off on it."

"Good. Because…" Lindsey spun them around, positioned Gia's back against the side of the pool, and pressed into her. "It's my turn to please you."

"I'm all yours." Gia was so excited, she'd almost come when Lindsey had, so it wouldn't take much to put her over the edge.

Lindsey sucked on her neck and positioned herself between her legs, causing Gia to sink lower in the water. Lindsey caressed her breast as she gently kissed her. "What do you want?"

"I want to feel you inside me," Gia said as she kissed her hard. Lindsey took a hand off Gia's breast, and her fingers tickled down Gia's abdomen until they settled at the desired location. "Go in," Gia groaned in Lindsey's ear as her breath caught. And hurry, she felt like adding. She had been on the verge of an orgasm since she'd started touching Lindsey, and the need to release was becoming more difficult to hold in. She wrapped her legs around Lindsey's waist and brought her hands behind her head to hold on to the edge of the pool as Lindsey thrust two fingers inside.

"I want to feel you come." Lindsey matched her rhythm, pushing deeper and with much more force.

Gia's weightless body moved with each thrust, splashing water over the edge of the pool. "Faster," she whispered. "Faster…yeah…yeah." She felt the pinch of Lindsey's warm wet hand on her nipple as she continued to thrust. That was all it took to release the explosion. She moaned deeply and tightened her thighs around Lindsey's body. It had been over five years since she'd felt the hands of another woman. No matter how many times she'd tried to convince herself that her vibrator provided the same pleasure, nothing compared to giving herself over to a woman's touch.

After a moment, the water stilled, and so did Gia's convulsions. "Damn," was all she needed to say as Lindsey smiled and nodded. She unwrapped her legs and let them float back to the bottom. She stood silent for a moment as she stared at Lindsey, then leaned in and hugged her. It was the first time she had been intimate since Audrey, and the depth of her feelings was causing her eyes to water. The blackmailer had turned to thief. Gia closed her eyes and held on tight to the woman who was rapidly stealing her heart.

They stayed in the pool for a while longer, talking and laughing until their skin turned wrinkly. "I think we should probably get out," Gia finally said.

Lindsey hopped on the ledge first. "Shit." She giggled as the water dripped off her. "The towels are up by the house."

"I'll go get them," Gia said as she pulled onto the ledge. The humidity that lingered in the air still felt warm on her skin.

"No, you might run into Jenn and Stacy." Lindsey grabbed her forearm.

"Do you really think they've even come up for air?" Gia had no doubt that Jenn's *tour of her house* consisted of only one room, the bedroom.

"Yeah, you're right. Probably not." Lindsey grabbed her clothes. "But I don't want to take the chance," she said as she attempted to get dressed.

Gia bent and did the same. They both twisted and turned as they tried to peel, pull, and tug their clothes over wet skin until they finally fell on top of each other, laughing. It took another several minutes and a helping hand from the other before they were completely dressed.

"I'll go grab the towels for our hair." Lindsey headed to the house.

"I'll come with you," Gia said.

"Well, well, well." Jenn announced from the porch. She was sitting next to Stacy on the swing, surrounded by what was left of Paul's three pies.

"Holy shit, you scared me," Lindsey said with a squeal. "I thought, um, I thought you two were…"

"Having sex?" Jenn put a hand to her chest. "I'm feeling insulted. Are you feeling insulted, Stacy?"

"Completely." Stacy smiled as she shoved a bite of pie in her mouth.

"But…" Gia trailed off as she cocked her head toward Stacy. This didn't make any sense. Normally, when Stacy was with a woman, she didn't come up for air for hours.

"I told you Jenn was giving me a tour. It's on you to have thought anything else." Stacy smiled.

"How much did you two—"

"See?" Jenn interrupted. "Enough to feel excited for both of you. Now come over here and join us. You'll need to put back some of those calories you just burned." Jenn handed them both a fork.

"Well, actually." Gia shuffled over. "Now that I feel completely embarrassed, a bite of pie does sound good."

"Don't feel embarrassed. I'm damn proud and happy for you," Stacy said as she hopped off the swing and hugged Gia. "Welcome back to the land of the living."

Jenn hugged Lindsey. "Me too, Linds, I was starting to really worry about you."

"You make us sound like we're total losers or something," Lindsey said as she sat on the porch and dug into the cherry pie.

"You were never a loser. You just lost something along the way. I'm really glad you found it." Jenn tried to mold Lindsey's hair, but Lindsey playfully stabbed at her with her fork.

Gia settled next to Lindsey and smiled. Yeah, she thought as she glanced over. She too had lost something along the way, and maybe through Lindsey, she had not only found it, but she'd promised herself that she would never lose it again.

CHAPTER NINE

With a smile on her face and happiness in her step, Lindsey pulled up in front of Paul's. She grabbed the tray of to-go coffees and a bag of scones. The front door was unlocked, so she let herself in. Paul was just starting to make a pot of coffee.

"Didn't you get my text?" she asked as she placed everything on the counter.

Paul looked at his phone. "What text?"

Lindsey dug out her phone and scrolled. "I sent you a text a half hour...oh, huh, looks like it didn't send. Oh well. Anyway, I brought coffee and scones. Are they up?"

"They're gone." Paul grabbed a coffee, took a sip, and moaned. "Oh, that's good."

"Gone, as in, out for a walk?" Lindsey popped a cup out of the tray.

"Gone, as in, they flew back to Phoenix."

Lindsey's knees began to buckle, and the walls felt like they were closing in on her. That was impossible. Gia would not have left without saying something. Especially after last night.

"Gia's mom called around two this morning. Her dad fell and is in the hospital. They woke me up, paid in full, then flew out the door. Gia was pretty upset when she left, but she told me she would call you later this morning and fill you in."

"Oh my God, is her dad okay?" She grabbed her phone and sent Gia a text.

He shrugged. "That's all I got. The rest you'll have to get from Gia."

She pulled out a barstool and sat. Visions of the frantic 9-1-1 call she'd made after her father had collapsed danced in her head. The despair that had gripped her as she sat with her mom in the waiting room. The minutes that had felt heavier as each ticked by and the words that had finally come from a doctor who could barely look her in the eye. She reached again for her phone, but Paul placed his hand over hers.

"Give her a moment, Linds. She said she'd call when she can."

She nodded as she released her phone. She had let Gia know in the text that she was thinking about her, and as helpless as that made her feel, right now, there wasn't anything else she could do except wait. She began sipping her coffee, her gaze faraway. "We, um, we kinda made love last night," she said in a distant voice.

The sound that came from Paul almost caused her to fall. "I fucking knew you two were right for each other the moment I saw you together. Jeff always says I have a sixth sense about things, and I was sensing it between the two of you big-time."

"I really like her." She felt the heat spread across her face as she grinned. Gia had opened something inside her, something she didn't want to let go of.

Paul came around and squeezed her tight. "Well, congratulations." He leaned out. "Jeff and I will be the first to come visit you in Phoenix."

Lindsey snorted. "I think a lot of things need to happen before either of us takes that step." She didn't want to leave everything and everyone to move for what might have been a fling. She needed to know that what had happened in the pool meant as much to Gia as it did her.

"Please, you've always wanted to get out of this town. Now's your chance. Besides, the moment I met Jeff, I knew he was the one. Love at first sight is a real thing, which is why I had no reservations when I asked him to move in with me."

"Yeah, but you guys dated for a year before he finally moved in." Her phone chimed. "It's a text from Gia," she said as she eagerly swiped her screen. "She said her flight's about to take off and she's sorry she hasn't called, but she's been on the phone nonstop with her mom. Her dad has two broken ribs and a fractured hip, and he's going into surgery now. She apologized for not being able to say good-bye and told me she'll call me once they land." Lindsey looked up. "She said she misses me already and ended the text with heart emojis."

He placed his hand on his chest. "Be still, my heart."

Lindsey nodded. After she'd dropped Stacy and Gia off at Paul's around midnight, she hadn't slept a wink, thinking about Gia's fingers inside her and her mouth on her breast. In just one night, Gia had managed to leave her footprints all over Lindsey's heart.

In an attempt to get a feel for where Gia lived, she and Paul googled Phoenix and studied photos and videos. By the time she downed the last of her coffee, she felt like she had a pretty good idea of the size and vibe of the place, and right now, she felt equal parts excited and terrified when she thought about moving to such a sprawling metropolis.

"Maybe Gia would consider moving here. She told me multiple times how much she loved seeing the green." Lindsey smiled at the thought.

"Maybe," he said with a shrug.

Lindsey felt a little lighter as her mind raced. She would talk to Gia about moving to Jacobe when the time was right. *Who knows, she just may say yes.*

❖

"Think she'll move to Phoenix?" Stacy asked as she buckled her seat belt.

Gia put her phone in airplane mode and shoved it in her purse. "Don't you think it's a little too soon to be talking about us moving in together?"

"Oh please, it's the first thought most lesbians have right after they cross the line. Look me in the eyes and tell me you haven't thought about it."

Gia grinned. Stacy was right. It was one of the first thoughts she'd had after they'd made love last night. In fact, other than her dad's fall, it was all she had been thinking about.

"Uh-huh, thought so." Stacy jabbed a finger at her.

"Okay, okay. I will admit, it's crossed my mind. And yes, I think it would be nice if she moved to Phoenix because I really can't see myself living in Jacobe. I mean, I enjoyed the place, and Paul and Jenn are wonderful, but it's such a small town." Although she had not taken advantage of the many things Phoenix had offer in the past five years, it was comforting to know that the sporting events, restaurants, art exhibits, and vibrant gay community were all there for her whenever she wanted to participate. If she moved to Jacobe, she feared she'd eventually get small-town fever and resent the move and eventually, Lindsey.

Stacy patted her hand. "I'm going to hold out hope that you two figure out a way back to each other. Meanwhile, I'm so proud of you." Stacy leaned over and kissed her on the cheek.

"How about you and Jenn? You two seemed to hit it off pretty good. Any thoughts of seeing her again?" For a brief moment, Gia entertained the idea of the four of them hanging out as couples. Logistically, it was an impossible dream but a fun thought.

"Well, after we had a little quickie in her house last night, we—"

"Shut the fuck up. I knew it." Gia smiled as she pointed at Stacy.

"Did you even doubt it for a moment?" Stacy teased. "Anyway, we're going to meet up at some yet undetermined place at some yet undetermined time and reconnect."

"Would you ever consider moving to Jacobe?"

"That's not where we're at. We both just want to have fun, and we're adult enough to call it exactly what it is. Finding forever isn't something either of us is looking for. At least, not right now."

"I can't do that." Gia could never understand how Stacy could be attracted enough to sleep with someone, yet not enough to want to be in a relationship with them. For her, the act of lovemaking was as much mental as it was physical. By the time she allowed someone to touch her body, she was well on her way to being in love. Unless the sex was god-awful, she knew by the time they finished that her emotions would already be in play.

"I know, which is what makes you, you and me...me."

Gia nodded as the plane ascended. She turned and looked out the window as the morning sun continued to rise over a sea of green trees. Somewhere down there was the other half of her heart. She closed her eyes and pressed her forehead against the Plexiglass. Funny, in less than three hours, she would be home, and the anxiety she'd had just days ago about leaving Phoenix, she now felt for returning. Everything inside her was aching to be in Lindsey's arms right now, to be held and soothed as Lindsey told her everything was going to be okay. She sighed. If only she had a few more days to get to know her better. To have the time to say the words welling up inside her. Words that really needed to be said in person. Gia opened her eyes as the clouds swallowed her view, and she wondered if Lindsey felt the same and if her heart already felt as broken as Gia's.

CHAPTER TEN

I got your card. But per your instructions, I haven't opened it yet."

Gia could hear the smile in Lindsey's voice, and it made her heart skip a beat. It had been two months since they'd made love in Jenn's pool, and the time away had been agony. Twice, she had booked a flight back to St. Louis but had to cancel both times when a situation came up with her parents. Between daily visits to the rehab facility to see her father, dealing with insurance claims, and making sure her mother's needs were met, Gia's life had become a whirlwind. "Good, because I want to be on the phone when you open it."

"Hi, Lindsey," Stacy said as she leaned toward the phone.

"Oh. Hi, Stacy." Lindsey called back. "Where are you guys?"

"We've been out running errands for Mom all morning. When we get back, Stace is going to help me install the grab bars for the shower. But right now, she's taking me to get some coffee because she says I'm looking haggard. Apparently, a caffeine buzz, over a good night's sleep, is the remedy."

"You've been burning the candle at both ends, and I've been more than a little worried about you," Lindsey said.

"I'll be fine. Did they…oh wait, hold on." Gia leaned across Stacy as she gave her drink order to the barista in the window. "Okay, sorry about that. I was going to ask, did they finish the roof yet?"

"They finished an hour ago, thank God." Gia heard the smile in Lindsey's voice. "Three days of listening to them bang away up there was starting to wear on my nerves. But it looks great. Now all I have left is the kitchen counter, and Jeff said he'd do that for just the cost of materials because I'm already way over my budget." Lindsey paused. "I really wish my parents were here to see how wonderful everything's turning out."

"I'm sure they're looking down from above and smiling."

"Yeah, I think so too."

"I can't wait to finally see it."

"Wait, are you telling me you booked another flight?" Linsey said as her voice raised an octave.

"Kind of. In fact, I think now would be a good time to open the card." Gia said.

"Okay, I'm opening it." Gia heard a ripping sound on the other end, then a gasp. "Oh. My. God." Lindsey squealed. "I, um, I don't know what to say." A louder squeal sent BeeBee barking in the background. "I can't believe you did this."

Gia had thought it was time they had a talk about their future. So she'd bought two round-trip tickets to LA. One from Phoenix, the other from St. Louis. A car was reserved, a weekend beach rental in San Luis Obispo was booked, and the itinerary had been sent to Lindsey.

"Say you'll meet me in California in two weeks. It's been too long since I've kissed those beautiful lips. And I'm so sorry that I haven't been able to get back there to see you."

"Nope," Lindsey said. "None of that. I told you, concentrate on your parents for now. I know how overwhelming something like that can be."

They'd ended up having to put four screws in Gia's dad's hip. After his third day in the hospital, he was transported to a rehab facility, where he'd spent the past several weeks being the biggest pain in the ass the nurses had ever dealt with. Four days ago, he was released, and Gia was sure the nurses heaved a sigh of relief.

"How's your dad doing?" Lindsey said.

"He's not using his walker around the house, we had to hide the car keys because he thinks he's perfectly fine to drive, and he doesn't want to take all his meds. Mom is about at her wits end with him and they're fighting more than I've ever seen."

"Well, that doesn't sound good. Hopefully he can…oh hey, can I call you back? Paul just walked in cradling a plant."

"Yep. Tell Paul hi. I'll talk to you later." Gia ended the call as she normally did, with a feeling of warmth in her heart and excitement for what lay ahead.

Stacy handed over a to-go cup. "You do know you get a pregnant glow every time you talk to her?"

Gia grinned and sipped her coffee as Stacy headed to the freeway. Gia glanced out the window and sighed at the latest wave of construction demolishing the desert to make way for more strip malls, tract homes, and mega apartment complexes. It was such a stark contrast from Jacobe. "Thanks again for helping me with the errands."

"It's the least I could do. You sounded so exhausted this morning."

"Yeah, I haven't gotten much sleep lately." She pressed against the seat, brought her knees to her chest, and put her feet on the dash.

"Why? Did something happen with your dad?"

"Actually." Gia took another sip and swallowed a lump in her throat as she turned away. "Something happened with Audrey. She contacted me two nights ago." Her stomach turned a bit sour as she thought about how Stacy was going to react. After all, it was Stacy who'd watched her wither away under Audrey's grasp.

"Thought you blocked her?" Stacy said in a dry tone.

"I did. She contacted me through *Gia's Gems*," she said, feeling apologetic but not really knowing why. It wasn't like she was the one who'd reached out. But still, she'd sworn to Stacy that she would never have anything to do with Audrey again.

"What did the weasel want?"

"To have dinner. She said she's been following my articles for a while and wanted to meet up, but she didn't say why."

"Please tell me you told her to get lost."

Gia didn't answer. Not only had she not told Audrey to get lost, she was actually entertaining the idea of having dinner with her.

"Damn it, Gia, after the way she treated you, are you kidding me?" Stacy grumbled as she changed lanes. "She's not your concern anymore. Don't go down this road. You've come too far. I'm telling you this as your best friend who loves you. Just because you two had a relationship doesn't mean you should feel obligated to be friends. You owe her nothing. I'm telling you, stay away from her. She's nothing but trouble."

"Don't worry, I'm not going to get caught up in any of her bullshit games. I've blown enough money on therapy to recognize the signs. I'll be fine." She awkwardly smiled as she took another sip and glanced out the window. But would she be fine? When she'd first read Audrey's email, a surge of unexpected anger had coursed through her veins and out her mouth. Why, after all these years of zero contact, did Audrey want to meet? She always had a self-serving angle, so what was her game? After Gia's third readthrough of the brief email, her mind went from anger to curiosity. Was Audrey sick? Had something happened to her? And therein lay the dilemma. If she didn't meet Audrey, and she was unwell in some way, Gia would always regret not seeing her, a guilt she really didn't want to bear. But there was something else. She ran Audrey's request by her therapist, who'd planted a seed in Gia's head. Her therapist had said that Gia still had unresolved feelings for Audrey, which was why she'd isolated herself so much after the breakup. When Gia had reminded her therapist how much she hated Audrey, her therapist had replied, "Love and hate are two faces of the same coin. All you have done is transfer the exact emotion to the other side."

Gia really didn't think that was the case. She was head over heels in love with Lindsey and having any feelings—much less lingering feelings—for Audrey just didn't make sense. But was her therapist right? Could she really look Audrey in the eyes and truly not feel anything for her?

"You going to tell Lindsey?"

"I don't know, probably not. I don't want her to jump to any conclusions. If I decide to be friends with Audrey, then I'll fill her in. If not, no sense worrying her over something that's a moot point." Gia thought about the jealousy she would probably feel if Lindsey said she'd accepted a dinner invitation from her ex.

Stacy frowned. "For what it's worth, I really think you should tell her, and also for what it's worth, I think you're making a big mistake if you agree to this dinner. Seeing that weasel will throw you in another tailspin. I finally have you back, and I don't want to lose you again."

"You won't. I promise."

Stacy grunted as she exited the freeway. "Tell Lindsey. Lying is what got you in trouble with her in the first place."

"I know, and I will. It's just that I want to meet with Audrey first and figure out what's up." Gia swallowed the last of her coffee. "And truthfully, I think there's a part of me that wants to meet because I want her to look me in the eye and apologize."

"And if she doesn't, will you crawl back into your hole?"

"I know what I'm doing, Stace, just trust me, okay?"

"Careful, Gia, you have a good thing with Lindsey, don't blow it."

"I'm not going to blow it." Gia huffed.

"Said every lesbian right before they did."

"Stop." Gia playfully slapped Stacy's shoulder. But she knew Stacy was right; she needed to be careful. Anything dealing with Audrey was playing with fire. She glanced at Stacy from the corner of her eye. There was something else she hadn't said, something she was too embarrassed to admit. Since Gia had been feeling so good these past few months, a petty part of her wanted to rub Audrey's face in it. Gia was in love, had a sexy new hairstyle, had trimmed down a bit, and was no longer a hermit. Her snarky side wanted to flaunt her stuff, let Audrey see what she'd thrown away so she'd hopefully wallow in regret.

Gia's phone rang. "It's Mom." Gia anxiously swiped the phone and hit the speaker. "Hi, Mom, we're almost home. Do you need us to pick anything else up?"

"Your father got stuck sitting on the toilet because he thought he didn't need to take his walker into the bathroom. He was stuck on that damn thing for an hour while I was at the grocery store. By the time I got back, his legs had fallen asleep."

"Why did you go to the grocery store? Mom, Stace and I have been out running around all morning getting everything on your list."

"You took too long."

"We've had to go to six stores to get everything you asked for." Gia pinched the bridge of her nose. "Anyway, we're almost back. Is Dad okay?"

"Well, I had to massage his legs until the circulation came back, then hoist him off the seat and onto the walker that should have been there in the first place. Now he has a nasty red mark the shape of the toilet seat on his butt that's not going away. But yeah, he's okay." She paused. "But you need to tell him he has to always have his walker with him. Henry!" Gia tapped the volume to a lower level. "Talk to your daughter."

"Hi, Gia."

"Hi, Dad, you really need to use your walker at all times."

"Horseshit to that," he replied.

"Give me that, give me that." Gia heard rustling and what sounded like slapping, then her mom came back on the phone. "Anyway," her mom groaned. "When you're done gaying around with Stacy, I'll also need you to scrape the hardboiled eggs off the ceiling."

"Mom, we're not gaying around. We're out shopping for you. And how the hell did hardboiled eggs end up on the ceiling?" Gia looked over at Stacy, who was cracking up.

"Before your father got stuck on the toilet, he decided to boil some eggs. When the water evaporated out of the saucepan, they exploded and are now all over the ceiling."

"I left you guys alone for what, three hours, and this is what happens? Mom, you have to keep a closer eye on him."

Her mom snorted. "Easy for you to say."

"Look, we're almost there. Just do me a favor. For the next five minutes, make sure Dad doesn't move."

"Okay, dear."

Stacy's cheeks were as red as a fresh sunburn. Tears were trickling down her face from laughter. "Your parents could star in their own sitcom. That was classic."

"Please shoot me if I ever get like that."

"Oh, honey, you and me both."

Gia had the sinking feeling that maybe it was time to have a talk with her parents about hiring a temporary caregiver to keep a watchful eye on her dad. She was sure he would resist the idea because he was too stubborn to admit he was at a point in his life where he needed help. She chuckled as she thought about the past five years of her own life in isolation and her own resistance to reach out for the kind of help she'd needed. "I guess the apple doesn't fall far from the tree, huh?" she murmured to herself.

CHAPTER ELEVEN

"Tell me again why sweating my ass off in here is any different than sweating it off outside?" Lindsey said as she lay opposite Jenn, wrapped in a towel on the wooden bench. Jenn had traded a cut and color for a thirty-day pass for two with the owner of Jacobe's newest gym, which featured a state-of-the-art dry heat sauna.

"Because this kind of sweat is supposed to relax and detox you."

"Well, I think I'm officially detoxed," Lindsey said as she sat up. "I don't think I can tolerate the heat any more. I'm hitting the shower."

"Well, look at it this way, it's preparing you for when you move to Phoenix." Jenn followed her out. "Have you told Gia yet?"

"No." The drop in temperature as Lindsey stepped into the air-conditioned locker room was a blast of relief. "I'm going to surprise her over dinner Friday night. She made reservations at some romantic restaurant on the beach, so I thought I would make a card and cut out a picture of me and BeeBee in the minivan and glue it on a map with an arrow that points to Phoenix."

"Okay, that's totally cute." Jenn stripped off her towel and stepped in the shower.

"Right?" In the past couple of months, Lindsey had become more convinced than ever that Gia was the one for her. They talked nonstop about anything and everything. They seemed to align with each other on all the important political and social topics that mattered, and she had not seen any red flags. She would miss Paul and Jenn, but the thought of a life traveling around with Gia made her heart soar.

"I'm going to miss you, but I totally get it. It's time you start living the life you always wanted. I haven't seen you this happy in a long time." Jenn called over the sound of spraying water.

Jenn was right; this was only the second time in Gia's life that she had felt so elated. In a few short days, she would be making love to Gia and discussing how they were going to merge their lives together. In fact, she was already going around her house, deciding what items she wanted to bring and which she wanted to sell. She couldn't wait to tell Gia that she was more than willing to move to Arizona and spend the rest of her life with her.

"How's it going with Stacy?" Lindsey asked as she emerged from the shower, grabbed a clean towel, and wrapped it around her.

"I never thought I'd say this but…" Jenn emerged and followed suit. "She's probably the most compatible woman I've ever been with." They made their way back to the lockers and dressed. Afterward, Jenn hovered behind Lindsey as she squeezed a dollop of gel in her hands. "Look up." She scrunched her hands through Lindsey hair as she pulled and positioned each strand. "I really love this cut on you," she said as her phone dinged. "Can you check that for me? It's probably Michelle needing something at the salon."

Lindsey glanced down. "It's from Cheryl. Looks like she sent you an attachment."

"Cheryl?" Jenn nodded toward her hands. "Would you mind opening it up? I don't want to get gel on my phone."

"Okay, but if it's a picture of her naked, I'm closing it down."

"Just open it."

Lindsey punched in Jenn's birthday, and a somewhat blurry but very recognizable picture of Gia having dinner with another woman filled the screen. Below it was a text: *Gia's out with her ex. Thought you said she was with your friend?*

Each word felt like a slap to Lindsey's face as she reread the text. With a swipe of her fingers, she enlarged the photo. Gia was dressed in a stylish, low-cut, black-sequin top. Her head was slightly tilted back in laughter. A gut-wrenching blow hit Lindsey's stomach, and she felt like the wind had been knocked out of her. Words gathered in her mind but died on her lips as she sat in stunned silence.

"Linds?" Jenn said. "What is it? What's wrong?" Lindsey turned the phone around. Jenn's brows shot up. "She didn't tell you?"

"No, she didn't." The words tumbled out of her mouth as numbness settled in. An old wound was ripped open, and a war began brewing inside her that pitted her past with the present.

"I'm sure there's a good explanation."

Of course there was a good explanation. But right now, she couldn't think of a single one. As she expanded the screen, she started feeling nauseous. All the reasons for seeing an ex hit her at once. *We needed closure. We needed to see each other one last time to know for sure. She just wants to be friends.* She had heard them all, and each one in their own right had merit. What she didn't understand was why Gia hadn't said anything about meeting up with Audrey. Why had Gia mentioned several times that she was going to her parents' house tonight but failed to mention having what looked like a romantic dinner with her ex? And that was what stung the most. *When people purposely don't bring something up, it's usually because they have something to hide.*

"You okay?" Jenn toweled the gel from her hands.

The words floated in the thick haze surrounding Lindsey's head, but she couldn't quite comprehend their meaning. "Huh?"

"I asked if you were okay?"

Lindsey blinked once. Twice. "Um. Yeah, sure. I'm fine." Complete sentences seemed to elude her as she swallowed the bitter taste of hurt.

"Uh-huh." Jenn sat next to her.

"Why didn't she tell me?" Lindsey mumbled as she continued to stare at the photo. Gia became Jasmine, and Audrey morphed into Brad. And Lindsey was once again an observer, watching all the promises that had been made crumble before her. "Please tell me that this isn't happening to me again."

"This isn't happening to you again. Look." Jenn leaned into her. "Gia isn't Jasmine, and we don't know the truth behind this picture. Maybe Cheryl got it wrong, and that's not Gia's ex."

"It is. I've googled Gia many times, and a few pictures of her and Audrey always pop up. Seems like I keep hearing about the lying side of Gia from your friend." The dryness in her mouth made each word hard to spit out.

"Gia didn't lie to you."

"We talked three times today. Am I to believe she just conveniently forgot about a date with her ex tonight?" Saying those words felt like a knife twisting in her heart.

"How are you going to handle this?" Jenn asked.

Tears sprang to Lindsey's eyes. "I'm going to handle it like any mature adult would. I'm going to have a meltdown."

"Linds..." Jenn reached for the phone. "Come on."

Lindsey twisted out of reach. "I'm sending this picture to my phone, then I'm going to send it to Gia's with a message."

"You do realize every time Cheryl has said something about Gia, you overreact and send her a message you end up regretting?"

"This is different."

Jenn snorted. "Really? How so?"

Lindsey wiped a tear and remained silent.

"Look, there was an explanation for what Gia did with her article, and there's an explanation for this."

"Hearing about everything after the fact is not how I want to do a relationship," Lindsey quietly replied as she handed the phone back, picked up her own, and typed. "There. I sent her the picture with my own caption." She sighed as the weight of hurt and rejection caused her shoulders to hunch.

"Well, yet again, I'm sure that will definitely get her attention."

Lindsey nodded. Why would Gia do that to her? She knew about her past with Jasmine. And to think she was going to move to Phoenix. Wow, what a mistake that would have been.

Jenn's frown was fixed when she glanced at Lindsey. "You better not be having a pity party in that head of yours. We'll figure this out. Now come on, let's go get a drink and talk about this some more. I need to replenish my electrolytes with vodka." She pulled Lindsey off the bench and draped an arm around her shoulder as they left the locker room.

Lindsey wiped away more tears. She was deeply in love with Gia, but she was not going to tolerate deception. She needed to have complete trust in her partner. No surprises and no omissions. This was something she would not give ground on. Granted, she'd easily forgiven Gia for her lies about the articles; that was somewhat understandable, and they weren't directed at her. This, however, felt like a direct assault not only to their relationship, but to herself.

Audrey picked a restaurant she and Gia used to frequent. "I haven't been here since we were together," Gia said as she sat. Her stomach was in knots, and she was feeling awkward, uncomfortable, and very self-aware. During their relationship, she had always seen herself through Audrey's critical eyes, and right now, all the self-doubt that used to consume her was creeping back.

"The menu has changed a bit, but other than that, it's about the same. I hope you don't mind." Audrey gestured to a glass of red wine. "Since I got here a little early, I ordered you a glass of pinot."

"No, that's fine. Thank you." Gia felt Audrey give her the once-over, which made her nervous. Did Audrey disapprove of how she looked? Or was it just the opposite? Yes, Gia had picked out a sexy top to wear, and yes, she'd spent time getting her makeup just right. But it was meant for show not to lure. She wanted Audrey to know how happy she was, and she wanted Audrey to regret their past. But as Gia took a sip of wine, it hit her how pathetic that seemed. How pathetic she seemed. Stacy was right, she should have told Audrey to get lost and been done with her. Revenge might have been a dish that was best served cold, but maybe it was even better not served at all.

As Gia watched Audrey look over the menu, Lindsey's smiling face popped in her head, and at that moment, she was sure of two things: she was more convinced than ever that Lindsey was the one she wanted to spend the rest of her life with, and it was past time to fire her therapist.

"You're, um…" They both said at the same time.

"Sorry, go ahead," Audrey said as she placed her menu on the table.

"I was just going to say that you're looking good," Gia awkwardly threw out as an icebreaker. Audrey did look nice tonight. She always did. That had never been a problem in their relationship.

"Thanks, and that's exactly what I was going to say. I really like your hair."

Gia wanted to snap that Audrey was the one who'd forbidden her from ever cutting it short. But through a calming breath, she reminded herself she hadn't come here to throw mud. "Shorter hair is so much more tolerable in the heat."

Audrey nodded as the server approached, took their order, and left. A moment of silence passed before Audrey spoke again. "I've been reading your articles in *L*. They're very entertaining. You've been to some pretty interesting places."

Gia snorted. *If she only knew.* "Thanks, and I heard through the grapevine you got married to…"

"Harper, yes we did. And did you also hear through the grapevine that we divorced six months ago?"

"No, actually, I hadn't heard that." The little karma devil on Gia's shoulder did a happy dance as she tried to maintain a neutral face. "What happened?"

"Apparently, she decided that she wanted to be back with her ex."

The karma devil was now doing a full-on jig, and her mouth twitched, dangerously close to giving away the giddiness she was feeling. "I'm sorry to hear that." She cleared her throat. "I, uh, I thought you two were happy."

"Well, thank you. I did too, but I guess not." Audrey frowned as she took a sip of wine.

Gia was gloating so much on the inside that if the dinner had ended at that exact moment, it would have been worth the price of admission. Gia decided to change the subject before she said something snarky. "Did you hear about my dad?"

"No, what happened?"

As Gia filled her in, they soon fell into an almost comfortable conversation. By the time the server cleared their plates, she intuitively knew her dinner with Audrey was just what she'd needed. The anger that she'd harbored for all those years, that she'd let cripple her into agoraphobic tendencies, were really hers to own. She'd used the excuse of a relationship that was bad from the start to be the face of the self-esteem problems that had rooted within her long before she had ever met Audrey.

Audrey just happened to be the person who'd triggered them. Bringing them to the surface in one big, fucked-up, tangled ball of dysfunction. And as the night lingered, Gia knew that although she no longer hated Audrey, she also didn't feel anything else for her. They had once shared a snapshot in time when their lives had overlapped, and it was nothing more than that. They might have had a past, but they would never have a future.

"I hope you don't mind me asking, are you seeing anyone right now?" An element of hope seemed to linger in the air. Was this what Audrey was asking, whether or not she was free to date?

"Well, actually, yes. I have someone special. Her name's Lindsey." Gia smiled as the countdown clock flashed through her mind. In just a few short days, she would be in Lindsey's arms, kissing her and talking about the possibility of moving to Jacobe.

"Oh." Audrey took a dramatic pause as she finished off her wine. "Really? Does she live in Phoenix?"

Gia shook her head. "No, out of state. And believe it or not, I'm thinking about moving so I can be with her." The look in Audrey's eyes said it all. Wow, had Audrey really set this dinner up with hopes of a second-chance romance? No news of an illness or an apology had surfaced yet, so maybe this was all about wanting a do-over.

"Moving? Really? Um, wow, where to?" Audrey asked.

"Missouri."

Audrey choked. "Missouri? As in, the Midwest?"

"Yep, that's pretty much where Missouri's located." Gia smiled, knowing full well the news about her wanting to move was probably blowing Audrey's mind.

Audrey scrunched her nose. "Why in the world would you move there?"

"Because that's where Lindsey lives. And that's where I found something I haven't felt in a long time."

"Oh yeah, and what's that?" Audrey asked with a bit of bite.

"My true self. I haven't felt that in a long, long—" Gia's phone notified her of a text, and she smiled. "It's Lindsey. Do you mind." She froze when she saw the picture of her and Audrey laughing at their table with the words, *Looks like your date with your ex is going well this evening.* As she reread the text, she could feel the venom dripping from each word. She spun in her chair as she scanned the restaurant.

"Who are you looking for?"

"I, um." Gia kept searching. If Lindsey wasn't there, then how did she get the photo? How was this even possible?

"Gia, seriously, what's going on?" Audrey asked.

Gia showed her the text.

"So?"

Gia couldn't believe what had come out of her mouth, then she remembered. *When you're in Audrey's orbit, it is* all *about Audrey.* "I, um, didn't tell Lindsey I was meeting you."

Audrey leaned back, raised a brow, and smirked. "Really? And why is that?"

Gia was reminded that Audrey was incapable of seeing anything besides her own reflection. "Because I didn't think…" She trailed off as she listened to the words come out of her mouth. That was just it, she hadn't thought. Or to rephrase that, she hadn't thought it through. But why would she? There was zero chance that Lindsey would know she was here, and she had every intention of telling her later this evening. And again, how the hell had she gotten this picture?

"Gia," Audrey said with a hint of annoyance. "Forget about her for right now. Let's order dessert and concentrate on us."

"Us?" Gia turned the word over in her head. "There is no us, Audrey."

"But I thought since you agreed to meet me for dinner, we could talk about having another shot."

Gia blinked. "I'm sorry, what?"

"I thought we could, you know, try again. I figured this dinner could be the start of a rekindling."

Gia swallowed a sarcastic snort. "Audrey, I could almost argue there was never an us. There was only a *you* in our relationship." She whipped out her credit card and handed it to the server as she approached. The need to call Lindsey was so overwhelming that her stomach was starting to cramp. "I spent the last five years wallowing in self-pity, living a totally secluded life, and spending way too much on therapy while you were off gallivanting in your new marriage. And now, some coward with a camera"—Gia took one last glance around the restaurant—"could ruin the one good thing that's come into my life." The server returned and handed Gia the black book. "The only *us* that we will have is a social media friendship at best. Now, sorry to be rude, but I need to make a call." Gia grabbed her purse and left Audrey looking stunned at the table.

By the time Gia hit the door, she was calling Lindsey. "Come on, Linds, pick up…pick up…pick up."

"Hi, this is Lindsey, leave a message."

"Linds, it's me. Call me back, okay?" Gia hung up and sent her a text to call her ASAP. She hustled to her car and sped toward home. What the hell had just happened? This morning, she was making mental plans to move to Jacobe, and tonight, she wasn't sure she still had a girlfriend. The first red light she came upon, she sent Stacy a quick text saying she needed to talk.

Stacy's reply was immediate: *I'm already at your house, see you when you get here.*

Gia didn't recall Stacy saying anything about coming over tonight. Not that it was unusual; they both had keys to the other's place, and it wasn't uncommon for one to pop in, but Stacy knew she was having dinner with Audrey tonight. As she pulled into her cul-de-sac, she saw Stacy's car in front of her house. Gia screeched into her garage, flew out of her car, and bolted inside.

"I'm in here," Stacy called out from the living room.

"Hey." Gia almost cried as she threw her purse on the kitchen island and shuffled into the other room.

Stacy sat on her couch, a glass of wine in hand. "I kinda started without you. Didn't think you'd mind."

Gia slumped next to her. "Someone took a picture of me and Audrey and sent it to Lindsey."

"I know all about it," Stacy said as she finished off her wine.

Gia stared. How could Stacy already know about the phantom picture? This night was getting weirder and weirder. "How?"

"Jenn. Seems we have a mutual friend. You remember Cheryl?"

She shook her head as her mind drew a blank.

"Claims adjustor, tall, blond, tan. We dated for a little while."

Gia hunched her shoulders.

"Ex-stripper."

"Oh yeah. Now I remember. But what the hell does Cheryl have to do with tonight?"

"Turns out, she and Jenn have a bit of the same history. And tonight, she was at the restaurant and saw you and Audrey. Guess Jenn had mentioned to her that you and Lindsey were an item, so she took it upon herself to send a picture to Jenn that said otherwise."

Gia now knew the *who* in the mystery. But she still had no idea about..."Why?"

"I don't know, sweetie. Cheryl's not the most mentally stable person. Great in bed, though."

Gia leaned forward and placed her head in her hands. Lindsey was her everything. She made Gia feel better about herself. Without her, Gia feared she would return to her isolated ways. "What am I going to do?" she asked desperately. "Lindsey won't return my calls or texts."

"I know, Jenn is with her now."

"Call Jenn."

Stacy held out her hand. "Hold on. First, tell me what happened tonight."

"Nothing happened." Gia sat back in her couch as Brody jumped on her lap. "I mean, at first, it was really awkward. Then we kinda got into a more relaxed mood when I told her about Mom and Dad. And then it was like, the more I talked to her, the more I realized how messed up that whole relationship was and how grateful I am to have someone like Lindsey. Seeing Audrey tonight made me realize how much I really do love Linds. Then I got the text, and I just freaked out. In fact, I rushed out of the restaurant and left Audrey sitting at the table."

Stacy chuckled. "Well, that's long overdue."

"I shouldn't have gone to see her, and I shouldn't have listened to my therapist. She told me I could be having unresolved feelings for her that needed exploring. But I'm telling you, every time I looked at Audrey tonight, all I could think about was Lindsey."

"How many times have I told you that your therapist is messed-up?"

"I know, I know, and I'm going to stop seeing her. But you know what's really weird? While I was sitting there tonight, listening to Audrey talk about *all things Audrey*, I realized our entire relationship had consisted of me trying to earn her approval. Not cutting my hair because she wanted me to look more femme, letting her pick out my clothes, allowing her to speak for me when we were out with friends. When I sat across from her tonight, completely untethered from her, I felt sorry for the old Gia who'd let herself become so lost in the eyes of a narcissist. It took seeing her tonight as the person I am with Lindsey to see that." Stacy leaned in and hugged Gia as she started to cry. "I'm in love with Lindsey, and I think I really blew it."

Stacy pulled out of the hug. "I know you are, and for what it's worth, I don't think you blew it." Stacy grabbed her phone and typed a lengthy text. "There," she said. "Let's just see, shall we?"

Gia was mentally kicking herself for not being upfront with Lindsey. She was desperate to explain herself. She needed to convey how much she loved her and that she was thinking about moving to Jacobe, all the words that she was going to say to her over dinner this Friday.

A few minutes later, Stacy was conveying Jenn's latest text. Based on Lindsey's mood, Gia needed to wait until Lindsey had calmed down a bit before trying to reach out. She nodded, let out a shaky breath and noticed the time. "Shit. I need to call Mom. I told her I'd swing by tonight, and I don't feel like being around them right now."

Gia made a quick call to her mom, who reassured her that she didn't need to come by. They were fine, her father was sleeping, and all was well.

As the night morphed into the early morning, the only ones communicating were Jenn and Stacy. By two o'clock, Gia passed out from too much emotional exhaustion and way too much wine. As tortuous as it was, the matters of her heart would have to wait another day to be resolved.

CHAPTER TWELVE

Tomorrow wasn't just Friday; it was *the* Friday. The day Gia had marked with a huge red heart emoji on her calendar app. She had thought by now she would be packing her bags for the romantic rendezvous in San Luis Obispo. Instead, she hadn't heard a word from Lindsey. Not a single text, call, or emoji. Nothing. Jenn had relayed that Lindsey just needed time and to not push it. Gia had told Stacy to relay back that she missed Lindsey with all her heart and that she was sorry.

"Stace, I was thinking about tomorrow," Gia said as she cradled her phone against her shoulder and walked across the parking lot to her car.

"Okay, first of all. Don't you dare think about bailing on me," Stacy barked. "And secondly, where are you right now? I thought you were at your parents' house settling in the caregiver."

"I had to go the store and pick up a refill for one of Dad's medications. I left her there to get more acquainted with Mom and Dad. Hopefully, they won't have run her off by the time I get back because I really like her. I think she'll work out just fine." Gia had talked her parents into hiring a full-time caregiver for the next few months, until her dad became a little more stable on his feet. Plus, having the extra help would benefit her mom and hopefully help ease some of the tension that had been brewing between her parents lately.

"Sounds like things are working out, so why the talk about wanting to bail on me?"

Gia let out a long sigh. "I'm not feeling all that well, and besides, you know what tomorrow is. I'm not sure I'm really up for going anywhere. I don't think I'll be good company." Yesterday, when it had become apparent that the trip to California wasn't going to happen, Gia had canceled the reservations, feeling dejected from lack of contact. Hours later, Stacy had announced that she'd booked a cute little cottage for them at a lakeside resort in Tennessee. She'd said that the distraction would do Gia good, and she'd refused to take no for an answer.

"First of all," Stacy said, "I know exactly what day tomorrow is, which is why you're going to get your sorry ass on that plane with me and go to Tennessee."

"I really don't feel well, Stace. Okay?" In the past few days, Gia had gone from hopeful to despairing, and the old feelings of wanting to hibernate were taking hold. She was shutting down in familiar ways as her past pattern started to emerge.

"No, Gia, I'm going to worry about you if you stay here this weekend. Now come on, you already agreed to this. Besides, you can use the place for your next *Gia's Gems* article. I know you have a couple of deadlines coming up."

"Here's an idea," Gia grumbled. "Why don't you go and send me back pictures like before?"

"No, we are not moving backward. You will be on that plane with me in the morning. Please tell me you didn't cancel Patty."

"I didn't." As much as it would sadden her mom, Gia didn't feel comfortable taking Brody over to her parents' house anymore. Having a pet sitter watch over him meant one less thing she had to worry about. "Okay, but I'm warning you." Gia sighed. "I won't be very good company."

"Well, then, I'll set my expectations to super low. There, the pressure's off." Stacy chuckled.

Gia huffed as she headed back to her parents' house. "What time's the flight?"

"Eight, so we need to be at the airport by six."

"Why so early?" Not that it mattered. Gia had been so upset lately, she was having trouble falling—and staying—asleep. Being up at all hours was sadly becoming her norm.

"It was the only nonstop. I'll pick you up at five thirty, we'll park in the economy lot, and take the tram over to the terminal. Easy peasy."

Gia surrendered. "Fine. But for the record, I really don't want to do this."

"Duly noted. Now go do what you need to do with your parents, and I'll see you in the morning."

Gia felt the sting of reality set in. She was supposed to be going to California to mark the start of a beautiful life with the woman she loved. How could one stupid misjudged moment cause all of that to come crashing down?

"What time did you say you wanted to leave tomorrow morning? I need to get BeeBee over to Paul's. He and Jeff are going to watch her while we're away." Lindsey grabbed the mug of coffee off the counter and followed Jenn. She sat in a high-back plush chair and set her mug on the small round table between them.

"The boys will spoil her rotten," Jenn said as she sat opposite and took a sip. "Oh, that's really good. I heard Frieda broke up with her coffee bean supplying boyfriend, and now he's selling to Masquerades."

"Who'd you hear that from?"

"Paul, who heard it from Jeff, who heard it from some guy at the gym," Jenn said.

"God, this town's gossip train travels fast." Lindsey took a sip and remembered the days when she was the lead story as that same train made its way around Jacobe. And the sting of the mumbled whispers and judgmental stares because of it. As much as the town's gossip was somewhat entertaining to partake in, being on the other end of it was brutal.

"Anyway." Jenn leaned back in her chair. "I was thinking if we hit the road around six, that should get us there around one."

Lindsey sighed. "I don't know, Jenn, I don't know if I—"

"Nope," Jenn interrupted. "I'm not going to hear it. You agreed to this, Linds, and besides, I've already put it on my credit card. If I cancel, I'll get hit with a huge fee. So, no, you are not going to complete that sentence."

"I was going to say, I don't know if I'm going to be very good company this weekend." Although she had picked up the phone to call Gia at least a hundred times, in the end, she'd held out on principle. She missed Gia with all her heart. She was the last image in Lindsey's head before she fell asleep and the first when she woke up to. But now, those images seemed to be fading in a cloud of numbness.

Jenn leaned over and kissed her on the cheek. "I always enjoy your company, and who knows, maybe this trip will spark a little life back into you. Besides, how long has it been since you were out of Missouri?"

Lindsey scoffed. "You know I've never been out of Missouri." And a sympathy trip to a cabin was not how she wanted to mark her first trip out of state.

"Exactly my point." Jenn regarded her. "Sweetie, Gia did say she was sorry, and according to Stacy, she sounds as miserable as you. You know, I bet you can still make your California trip if you just call and talk to her."

Lindsey held up her hand as if to say, don't even go there. Jenn, Paul, and even Jeff had all ganged up and tried to talk sense into her, but Lindsey was stuck in neutral. Jenn had said that fear of reliving old pain was clouding her vison for new love. Lindsey sighed. Maybe Jenn was right. Maybe this was still more about Jasmine than she wanted to admit. Deep wounds that she'd thought were healed but were apparently just scabbed over. Could she ever truly put the past behind her? *Not if it keeps getting dragged into the present.*

"Well." Jenn leaned over and patted her thigh. "Put it all out of your mind as much as possible. You and I are going on a road trip, and you're finally getting your ass out of here. And that, my dear, definitely calls for celebration." Jenn downed the last of her coffee.

Lindsey tried to muster a slight smile. "Do I need to bring anything in particular?"

"The brochure said there's plenty of hiking trails and water activities, so keep that in mind when you pack."

Lindsey nodded as she thought once again about Gia. She felt like she was at the intersection of *adventure* and *distrust*. And she had no idea which way she was going to turn.

❖

Gia leaned over Stacy and looked out the window as they were making their approach into Nashville International Airport. Although the fall foliage had only just started to turn and was still a few weeks from its prime display of brilliant oranges, yellows, and reds, Gia thought it looked magical. The desert never produced such a spectacular display of colors. To see that beauty, she would have to drive up north, to the high country.

Her mind drifted to Jacobe, and she wondered about its fall artistry. She thought about the large trees that framed the downtown area and wondered if they had already begun their winter hibernation. Her heart sank as her eyes began to water. Stacy had kept reassuring her that, according to Jenn, Gia just needed to hit the pause button for a little while longer while Lindsey worked through some old stuff. The adult in Gia understood, but the adolescent in her wanted to have a full-blown tantrum. Maybe after this weekend, she would go to Jacobe and throw herself at Lindsey's feet. She missed her, and she loved her, and that was all that mattered. Maybe it was time to make a Hollywood entrance and swoop in to get her girl back. Yes, she thought, that was exactly what she was going to do. Next week, she would fly to Missouri and surprise Lindsey. Gia smiled with anticipation as she leaned her head back, glanced out the window, and smiled at the possibilities.

The landing was as smooth as the flight, and after retrieving their overhead luggage and grabbing a well needed coffee, they followed signs to the rental car area. An hour later, they were headed toward Falcon Lake Resort. According to the GPS, they would arrive in two hours and thirty-four minutes.

But since Stacy was behind the wheel, Gia mentally shaved a good twenty minutes off that ETA.

As they drove through the lush winding hills, Stacy yammered on about the latest app her company was rolling out and what it would mean for the healthcare industry. Gia caught enough words to know when to nod or grunt, but her mind had already drifted to Lindsey. They would have been checking into their beachside rental right about now. She turned her phone over for the zillionth time. Still no messages or texts, and as for the heart emoji that marked this day on her calendar with such hope, she'd replaced it yesterday with the one that was broken.

As the tires crunched on the long gravel road that led to the resort, Gia powered down her window. The sun was warm, the air a bit cool, and the humidity, although thick, felt nourishing to her dry skin.

"Well, here we are." Stacy pulled up to the spacious, log-cabin style lodge and told her to wait in the car while she handled the check-in. That was fine by Gia because right now, she was tired and bordering on cranky. She had slept about three hours last night and not all at once. She yawned, reclined her seat, and looked at the lodge. It was cute in a woodsy kind of way, and she decided that Lindsey would have loved it. She leaned back and closed her eyes. The warmth of the sun shining on her face felt so nice, and she could feel herself losing consciousness as the visions and voices of a deep sleep rapidly took hold.

"I'm up for the Jet Skiing, but let's save the hike for tomorrow." Lindsey's voice worked its way into Gia's subconscious as she jerked awake. She blinked a few times and stretched as she tried to shake off the sleepy fog and rub the stiffness out of her shoulders. Her dreams about Lindsey were becoming more real.

Stacy came bounding back to the car. "We're all set, cabin number six." She looked at her. "You okay?" she asked as she turned over the engine.

"Yeah." Gia yawned again. "I fell asleep, and I woke to a dream about Lindsey talking about a Jet Ski."

"Well, that's not surprising," Stacy said as she moved the car down three cabins. "She's all you've been thinking about lately, and we did read that this place offered Jet Skiing."

"Yeah." Gia rolled out of the car. "I guess." But there was something about the voice she'd woken to that seemed so real. Gia shrugged it off. Stacy was right; her mind was probably playing tricks on her.

"Wow, this place is cute," Gia said as she opened the door. The cabin was floor to ceiling wood beams, the kitchen was modest, and although the furniture had seen better days, the worn-in look fit right in and added to the cabin's rustic charm.

"I'll take the loft," Gia said as she headed to a narrow staircase.

"You sure?" Stacy wheeled her luggage to the bedroom.

"Yep." Gia lugged her suitcase up the stairs and hoisted it onto a small dresser. "What's on the agenda for the remainder of the day?"

"We have dinner reservations at five thirty, so maybe between now and then, we can go on a hike." Stacy came out of her room while unfolding a map. "According to this, there's a trail that wraps around the lake. It's marked easy." She placed the map on the small kitchen table. "So that's a good thing."

"My kind of trail." Gia half-heartedly smiled. She was exhausted, and anything beyond a casual stroll didn't appeal to her right now.

Stacy called the front desk and asked what they should bring on this particular hike. The employee assured her that the path was smooth enough for flip-flops, and the only thing they needed was a bottle of water and a camera.

It took them a half hour to unpack and change. Gia grabbed her hat and sunglasses and signaled that she was ready. She set the pace at *easy stroll*. This wasn't about exercise; this was about getting out and enjoying the scenery, and to her delight, it was a spectacular view. Beautiful trees, that she identified only as green, outlined a small lake. A handful of people were standing on the shore with fishing poles in hand, a few small boats were in the water, and two Jet Skiers seemed to be racing to the other side of the lake. She released a long sigh and wondered what Lindsey was doing and hoped that whatever it was, she was enjoying her day.

"Beat ya," Lindsey called as she released the accelerator and let the Jet Ski idle. She shook the water from her hair and smiled for the first time in days. When Jenn and Paul had decided it was time for an intervention. Paul had suggested renting lesbian porn and eating sticky buns. Jenn, on the other hand, had proposed a minivacation somewhere out-of-state. And as she sat bobbing on the water while straddling the Jet Ski, she was glad Jenn's idea had won, even though she didn't totally rule out Paul's suggestion. Another day, perhaps?

Jenn pulled up next to Lindsey. "It's nice to see you smile again. I was starting to really worry about you."

Lindsey sat back. "Thanks. I think I really needed this."

"Well, what you really need, I can't give you, but I think this is a good start." Jenn smiled.

Lindsey chuckled as she glanced around the lake. It was a perfect day. The sky was crystal blue, the sun felt warm, and the temperature wasn't too chilly. She caught movement through a section of trees. She shaded her eyes, squinted at the two hikers bundled in sweats, and smiled. If Gia was here, she would probably be dressed like that too.

"Gia," Lindsey said softly as she closed her eyes. Gia was not Jasmine, and Lindsey was no longer a teenager. She would never be able to forget the past or completely conceal the scars she carried. But she realized she didn't have to. Like it or not, it was a chapter of her life that told a story of love and laughter and pain and heartache. And it was time she stopped going back and rereading those pages. Gia was not Jasmine, she repeated. Her story had yet to be told. And if Lindsey would just quit her knee-jerk reactions and stop throwing up blockades, maybe she could get out of the way long enough to let that chapter of her life write itself.

"I think it's time I give Gia a call," Lindsey said as she glanced at Jenn.

"Well, halle-fucking-lujah. It's about time." Jenn raised her arms in the air.

"Do you think it's too late? I mean, it still kinda fells like one big mess, but I want to talk to her. I really miss her." The word *miss* didn't even come close to the ache she had been feeling in her heart. In fact, she wasn't sure there was a word to describe the depth of such a hollow feeling.

"Messes can be cleaned up," Jenn said.

Lindsey nodded. Maybe after this weekend, she would fly to Phoenix and surprise Gia. Take her out to dinner and talk about everything this had triggered. Gia definitely had her flaws, but so did Lindsey. As long as they alternated their meltdowns, the relationship might actually have a chance.

"Come on," Jenn said. "I'll race you back to the other side. We still have another half hour on these things before we need to get cleaned up for dinner."

"Good, because believe it or not, I'm getting hungry." Lindsey hadn't had an appetite since this whole thing started. And now, with a plan circulating in her head, she was actually feeling invigorated.

"Well, tame the beast a little longer. Reservations aren't until five thirty. Last one back to the dock buys the first bottle of wine." Jenn squeezed the accelerator to full and let out a high-pitched squeal as her Jet Ski bunny-hopped across the water.

"First bottle?" Lindsey mumbled as she raced after her.

Gia looked up from the trail when she heard what sounded like a wounded animal crying out in pain. Upon further inspection, she realized the sound was coming from one of the two Jet Skiers out on the lake. As much fun as that looked, she couldn't imagine being out on the water in a swimsuit. She smiled as the float trip with Lindsey popped into her head, and sadness washed over her. What she would have given to have that day back.

"Watcha looking at?" Stacy stepped next to her.

"Jet Skiers." She pointed.

"Well, that looks like fun. Cold but fun. If they rent wetsuits, maybe we can go tomorrow?"

"You know what? I may take you up on that. It does look like fun." Gia placed her arm on Stacy's shoulder as they continued walking. It was time she embraced the fictional Gia in her articles. The one who was out enjoying life and was up for any adventure.

"How far do you think we've walked?" Stacy asked.

"I don't know. We're not even halfway around the lake, so I'd say probably about a mile or so." Gia regarded Stacy. "Why, are you tired?"

"A little bit," Stacy muttered as she rubbed the lower part of her back. "For the record, I think my outdoor endurance skills need some work. What would you say about heading back?"

"I'd say that sounds just fine with me." Being back out in nature and breathing the cool clean air had actually given her a second wind but not enough to override the fatigue of countless sleepless nights. Turning back was actually a relief. "Besides, this'll give us more time to shower and get ready for dinner."

"My thoughts exactly. We'll save checking out the other side of the lake until we're on something that has a motor and a bar attached to it," Stacy said.

Gia chuckled. Through the years, so many friends had told her and Stacy that they should get together because they fit so well. But that never made sense to them. They needed to stay in the role of best friends, where each could call the other out on their shit, provide support when one did something totally stupid, and be there to pick up the pieces when life shattered them. Their friendship might not have been of the intimate kind, but their love, appreciation, and trust for one another gave Gia exactly what she needed: someone who would stand beside her no matter what. And in exchange, she did the same for Stacy.

Two hours later, Gia checked herself one last time in the mirror. "Stace, it's almost five thirty, you about done in there?"

"I seem to be having a bit of a stomach issue right now," Stacy called from the bathroom. "Go to the restaurant, grab our table, and order me a glass of wine. I'll catch up."

"You sure? Because I can get something to go and bring it back. I'm fine with that." Gia thought eating in the room and watching a movie sounded more relaxing than dinner at the restaurant, anyway.

"No, no, just give me a minute. Go on without me. We have reservations, and I don't want them giving up our table. I'll be right there," Stacy said.

"Okay." Gia grabbed her purse. "Which name did you make the reservation under?"

"Just give them our cabin number. They'll know where to seat you. I requested a table by the window with a view of the lake."

"Sounds romantic," Gia softly said as she shuffled out the door. As she casually strolled to the restaurant, she wondered if the table for two that she had originally reserved for this evening was sitting vacant. Or if there was a couple who was appreciating the last-minute cancelation as they enjoyed a romantic dinner at the oceanside table. "We will be there one day, my love," she whispered as she opened the door to the restaurant. "I will do whatever it takes to get you back."

"Let me do that." Jenn grabbed at strands of Lindsey's hair.

"How do you do that so effortlessly?" Lindsey said as she checked herself in the mirror.

"What can I say, my fingers are the most gifted part of my body." Jenn smiled as her phone dinged. She wiped her hands on a towel, opened something, and typed for a moment. "Ready?" she said as she set the phone on the dresser.

"Yeah, everything okay?" Lindsey nodded to the phone.

"Yep, just, uh, a small issue at the salon. No biggie."

Lindsey wrapped an arm around Jenn's waist as they shuffled out the door. "Thanks, Jenn, I know I've been a pouty, grumpy, moody person lately, but I really enjoyed the day." When Jenn had picked her up this morning, Lindsey had been sitting on her couch in a mental fog, refusing to leave the house. Jenn had to drag her into her car. She barely remembered the first hour of the drive or what Jenn had been rambling on about. Her brain couldn't seem to process the fact that she was traveling east instead of flying west. Nothing seemed right, and she'd felt completely off balance.

Jenn kissed her head. "You're my bestie, and I love you. You'll get through this."

"Love you too." She leaned into Jenn.

"Oh shit." Jenn stopped walking and dug in her purse. "I left my phone on the dresser. Go ahead to the restaurant, and I'll meet you at the table."

"I'll wait," Lindsey said. She didn't really feel like walking into the restaurant by herself.

"No, no. Go snag our table and order me a glass of wine. We're already a little late."

Lindsey hesitated. "You sure? Because I can—"

"Yeah, no, really. Go on without me. I'll be right behind you," Jenn said. "Tell them your cabin number, and they'll know where to seat you."

Lindsey turned and walked backward a few steps. "Cabin number. Yep, got it." She glanced again at the lake and marveled at how beautifully the setting sun reflected off the water. She pulled out her phone and snapped several pictures. She wanted to send one to Gia and tell her she was finally out of Missouri and that she missed her, but instead, she shoved her hands in her front pockets. Better yet, she decided, she would show the pics to Gia in person next week when she flew to Phoenix to surprise her. Yes, Lindsey thought as she picked up the pace, it was finally time to close the doors on her past and open the most important one. The one that led to her future.

"Hi." She smiled as she approached the hostess. "Reservation for cabin number ten."

"Ah, yes, right this way."

The restaurant was framed by floor to ceiling windows, which offered a perfect view of the lake. Tables were draped in white linen, accented with a candle, and each had a vase of beautiful flowers. The sound of crackling logs made her turn toward an oversized stone fireplace against the far wall. The restaurant was not only beautiful, it was romantic. As the server guided her through the maze of tables, the glare from the setting sun momentarily blinded her. She almost collided with the server.

"Here you go. Enjoy your dinner," the server said as she stepped back and around her.

Lindsey's brows shot up, and her pulse quickened as she gasped. How was this even possible? In her stomach, a combination of excitement and apprehension mixed. She did not reach out or move at all. She stood in a stunned haze as words filled her heart but her mouth was too dry to speak them.

❖

"Lindsey?" Gia's heart jumped. Warmth filled her chest and heated her cheeks. "What, um, what are you doing here?" She fought the urge to pull Lindsey into a tight embrace, to passionately kiss her and tell her how sorry she was and how much she'd missed her. But Lindsey's body language seemed a bit standoffish, so she reluctantly kept herself rooted in her seat. She had a dozen questions, and each came with a different set of emotions.

"I'm here with Jenn. She thought it would be good for me to get away this weekend, so she booked us a cabin. In fact, she's about to join me. What are you doing here? And who are you with?" Lindsey's tone seemed a bit accusatory as she glanced at the two glasses of wine sitting on the table.

"I'm here with Stacy. Who, coincidently, also booked a cabin two days ago when it was apparent we weren't going to meet up in California," Gia said as her mind began connecting the dots. She didn't know whether to be pissed or elated that Stacy and Jenn had done this, and she pulled her phone from her purse.

"Yeah?" Stacy answered, out of breath.

"Hi, Stace. Funny thing…I'm here with Lindsey right now. Care to enlighten us?" Gia asked as she gazed at Lindsey. She was wearing black jeans and a light blue sweater that accentuated her eyes. It had been two long months since they had been together, and it was close to impossible not to reach out and touch her. To gently cup her face, pull her close, and kiss her deep. All she needed was a sign from Lindsey that she had been forgiven. Just one sign and she could release the knot in her stomach and breathe a sigh of relief.

"Look...Jenn and I just thought the two of you seemed to be...in so much pain without each other. What harm could there be in bringing...you together," Stacy said in fragmented sentences as she breathed heavily. "Enjoy your dinner...and we'll talk about it in a bit," Stacy groaned. "But not right now...in fact, don't come back to the cabin for an hour." The line went dead.

"Stace. Stace?" Gia looked over at Lindsey, took a deep breath, and placed the phone on the table. She wasn't sure how Lindsey would take the news, but no matter what, she was grateful the outcome of this little scheme had pushed them together. "As I'm sure you've figured out by now, we've been set up. And not only that, I'm banned from my cabin for an hour." Gia timidly glanced at Lindsey and waited for either anger or amusement.

"Those two aren't..."

"Oh yes, they are." Gia smiled as her gaze once again traveled to Lindsey's for answers. When none came, she broke the ice between them. "Lindsey, I um...will you please join me for dinner?" She held her breath as Lindsey paused, looked around, then nodded. Gia exhaled a sigh of relief as Lindsey pulled out the chair and took a seat. "First of all, wow, look at you. You're finally out of Missouri."

"I am." Lindsey smiled.

"Congratulations Linds. And I know this isn't quite the maiden voyage we both had envisioned for your first adventure out-of-state. And I'm so sorry," she said with a shaky voice. "Linds, I—"

"Gia." Lindsey cut her off. "I need to say something."

"Oh. Okay." Gia lowered her head as her stomach tightened. Lindsey was about to officially break it off, she could feel it in her bones. She'd fucked up, and she was about to pay the price. Did she regret seeing Audrey? No. That night had brought her needed clarity. The regret came from not sharing her reasons with Lindsey. It was selfish on her part and a lesson she wished she'd never had to learn.

"Gia," Lindsey said in a soft voice. "I need you to look at me."

"Do I have to?" Gia said as she squirmed. Hearing the words would be bad enough. Looking Lindsey in the eye while she said them would be a pain she didn't want to endure.

"Yes," Lindsey firmly replied.

Gia slowly lifted her head and focused on the one person she wanted more than anything else in her life. Lindsey made her feel so complete, she feared she would revert back to total isolation without her. "Okay. I'm listening."

Lindsey placed her hands on the table, palms up, and gestured for Gia to place her hands on hers. As soon as Gia's fingers glided over Lindsey's palms, she shivered from the electric pulse between them. The tears she had been holding back released, and she began to cry. This wasn't how she'd wanted it to end between them, and she only had herself to blame.

"Are you okay?" Lindsey squeezed her hand.

"No, I'm not okay. I've been a wreck these past few days. I'm so sorry for not telling you up front about Audrey. I thought you would think I was being petty and ridiculous because a part of the reason I'd agreed to meet her that night was to flaunt how happy I was with you. I wanted her to regret what she did, and I was embarrassed to admit it. I was going to tell you about it when we talked that night, but then..." She released her one hand and wiped away a tear. "But then, everything went wrong. I don't regret seeing her that night because it really hammered that last nail in the coffin of who we once were. But I truly regret not telling you up front. Stacy told me I should, but I just…I just…" Gia choked. "The thought of never seeing you again or kissing you has ripped my heart apart. I'm so sorry," she said as tears dripped onto the tablecloth. "I'm so sorry," she barely choked out.

They sat for a silent moment, staring at each other. Say something, Gia felt like pleading. *Please just say something.*

Lindsey leaned over the table and kissed her passionately. When Lindsey broke the kiss, she grabbed a glass of wine. "I want to…" She raised her glass. "Share with you something I was prepared to say at the restaurant in California. I think it's even more appropriate now." She cleared her throat. "Gia, my love. Here's to new beginnings, open doors, chapters yet to be written, and a life full of travel and adventure, fueled by…" Lindsey trailed off as she arched a seductive brow. "A love that never dies."

"You're not…" Gia wiped another tear from her cheek. "You're not breaking up with me?"

"Not even close." Lindsey grinned. "Did, um, did I ever tell you I still troll my ex's social media page and may or may not throw food at the computer when I see happy pictures of her and her husband? You're not the only one who has petty thoughts when it comes to their ex."

Gia chuckled as she dabbed under her eyes. The muscles she had been tensing finally relaxed, and her stomach calmed from the roller coaster ride of emotions. They were still together; she smiled at that acknowledgment as she made a promise to herself. No matter what happened in her life, from the insignificant to the substantial, Lindsey would be a part of it all. Sharing a life with her meant sharing all of her. Even the things that seemed embarrassingly petty.

For the next hour, they talked nonstop about each other's expectations and what they needed and wanted in the relationship going forward. And as the sun set on the lake, and the outside torches were lit, Gia smiled. This was not the location she had hoped for this weekend, but it sure delivered on the most important element. It brought them back together, and the rest, she knew, would work itself out in time.

As they were finishing their dessert, Jenn and Stacy shuffled over and took the empty seats next to them.

"Hi, Gia," Jenn said as she sat next to Lindsey. "Fancy meeting you here." She grabbed Lindsey's spoon and dug into the cheesecake.

Stacy sat next to Gia, placed her arm around her shoulder, and leaned in. "You doing okay?"

Gia nodded. "Very."

"Okay, ladies," Jenn said. "What's good here? We're starving."

"Lindsey had their everything salad, and I ordered the mushroom carbonara pasta, which was amazingly good," Gia mumbled as she ate as spoonful of ice cream.

"And this delicious dish, what is this?" Jenn pointed to Lindsey's plate.

"Chocolate chip cookie-dough cheesecake with vanilla ice cream and walnuts," Lindsey answered.

Jenn scooped a bit and lifted the spoon to Stacy's mouth. "Try this, sweetheart."

Gia and Lindsey both mouthed the word *sweetheart* to each other and grinned.

"Oh my God, that's good," Stacy moaned as the server walked over.

"Dave," Gia introduced. "These are our fashionably late friends, Jenn and Stacy."

He smiled as he handed out menus. "Very nice to meet you, what can I get you to drink?"

"I love a person who has their priorities in order," Jenn said. "Do you have a red wine that you suggest?"

"The house pinot is really good," he said.

Jenn looked to Stacy, who nodded. "We'll both have that. Now…" She waved a finger at Gia and Lindsey. "Let's talk cabins." She dug in her purse and pulled out her key.

Dave returned with two glasses of wine and a basket of warm rolls.

"Dave, honey, I can already tell by the size of this glass that we'll need another one right behind this one." Jenn waved toward the glasses, then turned to Gia and Lindsey. "Now then, Stacy and I were thinking how nice it would be to be able to share the same cabin. That means you two semi-functioning adults will have to figure out a way to cohabitate for the next two days while you let your best friends enjoy each other. Here's my key." She handed it to Gia. "I already moved my stuff over to your cabin, so all you need to do is move your things to Lindsey's." Jenn turned and winked at Lindsey. "Now, go help Gia move her things and enjoy the rest of your evening while Stacy and I eat and catch up."

"But—" Lindsey began.

"No buts, and don't worry about the bill, I'll handle it. Now go on. Shoo." Jenn waved them on.

Gia smiled as she got up from the table. "I think that's our cue to leave."

"Perceptive, that one is." Jenn laughed as she nodded at Gia.

"All right, then." Lindsey got up and began walking away from the table. "Guess I'll see you whenever."

Jenn smiled. "I think that timeframe works perfectly."

❖

"You sure you're okay with me moving into your cabin?" Gia asked as she rolled her suitcase behind Lindsey. She needed Lindsey to tell her that everything between them was okay. She didn't want to be sharing the same space with her and think for a single moment that Lindsey had any lingering resentment.

Lindsey stopped and turned. She placed her hands behind Gia's neck and pulled her in for a long soft kiss. It was the unspoken words of passion, and it left no doubt in Gia's mind where she stood. When they broke, Gia leaned in and whispered, "Wanna go make up for lost time?"

"Funny." Lindsey entwined their fingers. "I was just thinking that same thing." She led Gia into her cabin. "You can put your suitcase over there for now." Lindsey pointed to the far corner.

"Your cabin looks just like…" Gia stopped as she turned. Lindsey was lying topless on the bed and was just beginning to unzip her jeans. "You, um…" Gia licked her lips as she felt her nipples harden. "You don't waste any time, do you?"

"I've wasted enough time. Now come here, I want to feel you," Lindsey said in a soft voice.

"Yes, ma'am." Gia grinned and approached the bed. She could already feel the wetness building between her legs as she kneeled on the mattress. She crawled to Lindsey and swung one leg over to straddle her.

"Better not be thinking of keeping those clothes on for very long. When I said I wanted to feel you, I meant naked and wet," Lindsey said.

Gia rolled off and wiggled out of her clothes. "Better?" She rolled back on top, and their bodies fused into one.

"Much," Lindsey moaned.

"Now," Gia whispered as she began gently grinding into Lindsey and kissing her neck. "Since we just passed our two-month *sexiversary*, what do you..." Gia licked down Lindsey's neck to her breast. "What do you suggest we do to mark the momentous milestone?"

"We could always..." Lindsey barely whispered as she arched her back. "Skinny-dip in the lake to recreate our first night together?"

Gia playfully bit Lindsey's nipple, causing her to moan. "I think for tonight, let's stay dry, warm, and limber." She began licking her way down Lindsey's stomach.

Lindsey wrapped her legs around Gia's shoulders. "Good call, babe."

Babe. The word echoed in Gia's head as she settled between Lindsey's legs. Funny how that one word defined so much between two people. "Babe," Gia whispered back, "I love you."

Epilogue

One year later

"Ready, babe?" Gia called as she finished packing the conversion van. They were headed to California to spend a leisurely month driving up the coast. She thought it past time that Lindsey experienced the place that had once held so many of her dreams.

"Yep, coming!" Lindsey dashed out of her house with BeeBee in the lead.

"Everything locked up?" Gia asked as she placed a couple boogie boards in the back of the van.

"Yep." Lindsey grunted as she slid the side door open. BeeBee jumped in and settled into her dog bed. Seven months ago, Gia had sold her house in Phoenix, bought the van, and moved her and Brody to Jacobe. Into Lindsey's house, to be more precise. The cost of living was so much cheaper that the money Gia had made from the sale would carry them both for quite a while.

"Did you call your mom?" Lindsey asked.

"She was on her way to brunch with her book club. She said to tell you hi." The temporary caregiver was now a permanent hire. Having someone watch over her dad and entertain him was a taste of freedom Gia's mom didn't want to let go. The calls between them were still frequent, but her mom's yelling had been replaced with lighthearted stories of all the things she did each day. Something Gia, and her hearing, were grateful for.

She'd changed her website from *Gia's Gems, the Adventures of a Single, Thirty-something Lesbian* to *Gia and Lindsey's Travel Adventures*. The column's readership continued to expand, and she'd recently signed contracts with two mid-sized sponsors.

"Are you positive Jenn's good with taking care of Brody for this long?" Gia asked as she backed out of the driveway.

"Are you kidding? Jenn and that cat are reenacting some weird, past life relationship thing. It's like they can't get enough of each other."

"Well, he's good company for her while Stacy's away." In a move that shocked everyone, Stacy and Jenn had gone for a wild weekend in Las Vegas and had come back married. Since Stacy could live anywhere, but Jenn was tethered to her salon, Jacobe seemed the logical choice. The four of them, plus Paul and Jeff, had become inseparable. Gia had never felt so loved or so at home in her life.

As Gia pulled up in front of Paul's, Lindsey sent a text. Within seconds, Paul came bounding out of the house and down the walkway. His right arm was in a sling, and his left arm tightly gripped two plastic containers.

Lindsey powered down her window. "Holy shit, Paul, what happened?"

"I tripped over the drill's power cord when I was helping Jeff build a bookcase. I have a hairline fracture in my elbow."

"Oh my God, that sounds awful," Gia said as she leaned over.

"It is. But at least I got injured doing something butch instead of something in the kitchen, like usual." Paul handed over the containers. "The pink container is the pasta dish, and the blue one is the potato salad. Jeff said it's my best yet, so you'll have to let me know what you think."

Lindsey placed both in the cooler that sat between them. "Thanks, see you next month." Lindsey leaned out and kissed him on his cheek.

"Have fun, you two," he said.

"We will." Gia smiled. "And thanks again for the food."

"Oh please. It's the least I could do." His business had more than tripled since Gia's article on Jacobe was published. The extra revenue allowed him to lease a space downtown and turn it into a bakery. The sticky buns Gia had mentioned in her column were in such high demand, he was shipping them around the country.

As they drove away, Gia glanced over as Lindsey leaned into the wind. A tingle shot up her body as she smiled at the woman who held her heart so completely. And to think, all it took was a dose of good old-fashioned blackmail.

About the Author

Toni Logan grew up in the Midwest but soon transplanted to the land of lizards and saguaro cactus. She loves hanging out with friends, eating insanely delicious vegan food, traveling to the beach (any beach), and hiking in the mountains. She shares her Arizona home with a terrier mix who thinks she's a queen and four rescued cats.

Books Available from Bold Strokes Books

A Convenient Arrangement by Aurora Rey and Jaime Clevenger. Cuffing season has come for lesbians, and for Jess Archer and Cody Dawson, their convenient arrangement becomes anything but. (978-1-63555-818-0)

An Alaskan Wedding by Nance Sparks. The last thing either Andrea or Riley expects is to bump into the one who broke her heart fifteen years ago, but when they meet at the welcome party, their feelings come rushing back. (978-1-63679-053-4)

Beulah Lodge by Cathy Dunnell. It's 1874, and newly engaged Ruth Mallowes is set on marriage and life as a missionary... until she falls in love with the housemaid at Beulah Lodge. (978-1-63679-007-7)

Gia's Gems by Toni Logan. When Lindsey Speyer discovers that popular travel columnist Gia Williams is a complete fake and threatens to expose her, blackmail has never been so sexy. (978-1-63555-917-0)

Holiday Wishes & Mistletoe Kisses by M. Ullrich. Four holidays, four couples, four chances to make their wishes come true. (978-1-63555-760-2)

Love By Proxy by Dena Blake. Tess has a secret crush on her best friend, Sophie, so the last thing she wants is to help Sophie fall in love with someone else, but how can she stand in the way of her happiness? (978-1-63555-973-6)

Loyalty, Love, & Vermouth by Eric Peterson. A comic valentine to a gay man's family of choice, including the ones with cold noses and four paws. (978-1-63555-997-2)

Marry Me by Melissa Brayden. Allison Hale attempts to plan the wedding of the century to a man who could save her family's business, if only she wasn't falling for her wedding planner, Megan Kinkaid. (978-1-63555-932-3)

Pathway to Love by Radclyffe. Courtney Valentine is looking for a woman exactly like Ben—smart, sexy, and not in the market for anything serious. All she has to do is convince Ben that sex-without-strings is the perfect pathway to pleasure. (978-1-63679-110-4)

Sweet Surprise by Jenny Frame. Flora and Mac never thought they'd ever see each other again, but when Mac opens up her barber shop right next to Flora's sweet shop, their connection comes roaring back. (978-1-63679-001-5)

The Edge of Yesterday by CJ Birch. Easton Gray is sent from the future to save humanity from technological disaster. When she's forced to target the woman she's falling in love with, can Easton do what's needed to save humanity? (978-1-63679-025-1)

The Scout and the Scoundrel by Barbara Ann Wright. With unexpected danger surrounding them, Zara and Roni are stuck between duty and survival, with little room for exploring their feelings, especially love. (978-1-63555-978-1)

Bury Me in Shadows by Greg Herren. College student Jake Chapman is forced to spend the summer at his dying grandmother's home and soon finds danger from long-buried family secrets. (978-1-63555-993-4)

Can't Leave Love by Kimberly Cooper Griffin. Sophia and Pru have no intention of falling in love, but sometimes love happens when and where you least expect it. (978-1-636790041-1)

Free Fall at Angel Creek by Julie Tizard. Detective Dee Rawlings and aircraft accident investigator Dr. River Dawson use conflicting methods to find answers when a plane goes missing, while overcoming surprising threats, and discovering an unlikely chance at love. (978-1-63555-884-5)

Love's Compromise by Cass Sellars. For Piper Holthaus and Brook Myers, will professional dreams and past baggage stop two hearts from realizing they are meant for each other? (978-1-63555-942-2)

Not All a Dream by Sophia Kell Hagin. Hester has lost the woman she loved and the world has descended into relentless dark and cold. But giving up will have to wait when she stumbles upon people who help her survive. (978-1-63679-067-1)

Protecting the Lady by Amanda Radley. If Eve Webb had known she'd be protecting royalty, she'd never have taken the job as bodyguard, but as the threat to Lady Katherine's life draws closer, she'll do whatever it takes to save her, and may just lose her heart in the process. (978-1-63679-003-9)

The Secrets of Willowra by Kadyan. A family saga of three women, their homestead called Willowra in the Australian outback, and the secrets that link them all. (978-1-63679-064-0)

Trial by Fire by Carsen Taite. When prosecutor Lennox Roy and public defender Wren Bishop become fierce adversaries in a headline-grabbing arson case, their attraction ignites a passion that leads them both to question their assumptions about the law, the truth, and each other. (978-1-63555-860-9)

Turbulent Waves by Ali Vali. Kai Merlin and Vivien Palmer plan their future together as hostile forces make their own plans to destroy what they have, as well as all those they love. (978-1-63679-011-4)

Unbreakable by Cari Hunter. When Dr. Grace Kendal is forced at gunpoint to help an injured woman, she is dragged into a nightmare where nothing is quite as it seems, and their lives aren't the only ones on the line. (978-1-63555-961-3)

Veterinary Surgeon by Nancy Wheelton. When dangerous drugs are stolen from the veterinary clinic, Mitch investigates and Kay becomes a suspect. As pride and professions clash, love seems impossible. (978-1-63679-043-5)

A Different Man by Andrew L. Huerta. This diverse collection of stories chronicling the challenges of gay life at various ages shines a light on the progress made and the progress still to come. (978-1-63555-977-4)

All That Remains by Sheri Lewis Wohl. Johnnie and Shantel might have to risk their lives—and their love—to stop a werewolf intent on killing. (978-1-63555-949-1)

Beginner's Bet by Fiona Riley. Phenom luxury Realtor Ellison Gamble has everything, except a family to share it with, so when a mix-up brings youthful Katie Crawford into her life, she bets the house on love. (978-1-63555-733-6)

Dangerous Without You by Lexus Grey. Throughout their senior year in high school, Aspen, Remington, Denna, and Raleigh face challenges in life and romance that they never expect. (978-1-63555-947-7)

Desiring More by Raven Sky. In this collection of steamy stories, a rich variety of lovers find themselves desiring more, more from a lover, more from themselves, and more from life. (978-1-63679-037-4)

Jordan's Kiss by Nanisi Barrett D'Arnuck. After losing everything in a fire, Jordan Phelps joins a small lounge band and meets pianist Morgan Sparks, who lights another blaze, this time in Jordan's heart. (978-1-63555-980-4)

Late City Summer by Jeanette Bears. Forced together for her wedding, Emily Stanton and Kate Alessi navigate their lingering passion for one another against the backdrop of New York City and World War II, and a summer romance they left behind. (978-1-63555-968-2)

Love and Lotus Blossoms by Anne Shade. On her path to self-acceptance and true passion, Janesse will risk everything—and possibly everyone—she loves. (978-1-63555-985-9)

Love in the Limelight by Ashley Moore. Marion Hargreaves, the finest actress of her generation, and Jessica Carmichael, the world's biggest pop star, rediscover each other twenty years after an ill-fated affair. (978-1-63679-051-0)

Suspecting Her by Mary P. Burns. Complications ensue when Erin O'Connor falls for top real estate saleswoman Catherine Williams while investigating racism in the real estate industry; the fallout could end their chance at happiness. (978-1-63555-960-6)

Two Winters by Lauren Emily Whalen. A modern YA retelling of Shakespeare's *The Winter's Tale* about birth, death, Catholic school, improv comedy, and the healing nature of time. (978-1-63679-019-0)

Busy Ain't the Half of It by Frederick Smith and Chaz Lamar Cruz. Elijah and Justin seek happily-ever-afters in LA, but are they too busy to notice happiness when it's there? (978-1-63555-944-6)

Calumet by Ali Vali. Jaxon Lavigne and Iris Long had a forbidden small-town romance that didn't last, and the consequences of that love will be uncovered fifteen years later at their high school reunion. (978-1-63555-900-2)

Her Countess to Cherish by Jane Walsh. London Society's material girl realizes there is more to life than diamonds when she falls in love with a non-binary bluestocking. (978-1-63555-902-6)

Hot Days, Heated Nights by Renee Roman. When Cole and Lee meet, instant attraction quickly flares into uncontrollable passion, but their connection might be short lived as Lee's identity is tied to her life in the city. (978-1-63555-888-3)

Never Be the Same by MA Binfield. Casey meets Olivia and sparks fly in this opposites attract romance that proves love can be found in the unlikeliest places. (978-1-63555-938-5)

Quiet Village by Eden Darry. Something not quite human is stalking Collie and her niece, and she'll be forced to work with undercover reporter Emily Lassiter if they want to get out of Hyam alive. (978-1-63555-898-2)

Shaken or Stirred by Georgia Beers. Bar owner Julia Martini and home health aide Savannah McNally attempt to weather the storms brought on by a mysterious blogger trashing the bar, family feuds they knew nothing about, and way too much advice from way too many relatives. (978-1-63555-928-6)

The Fiend in the Fog by Jess Faraday. Can four people on different trajectories work together to save the vulnerable residents of East London from the terrifying fiend in the fog before it's too late? (978-1-63555-514-1)

The Marriage Masquerade by Toni Logan. A no strings attached marriage scheme to inherit a Maui B&B uncovers unexpected attractions and a dark family secret. (978-1-63555-914-9)

Flight SQA016 by Amanda Radley. Fastidious airline passenger Olivia Lewis is used to things being a certain way. When her routine is changed by a new, attractive member of the staff, sparks fly. (978-1-63679-045-9)

Home Is Where the Heart Is by Jenny Frame. Can Archie make the countryside her home and give Ash the fairytale romance she desires? Or will the countryside and small village life all be too much for her? (978-1-63555-922-4)

Moving Forward by PJ Trebelhorn. The last person Shelby Ryan expects to be attracted to is Iris Calhoun, the sister of the man who killed her wife four years and three thousand miles ago. (978-1-63555-953-8)

Poison Pen by Jean Copeland. Debut author Kendra Blake is finally living her best life until a nasty book review and exposed secrets threaten her promising new romance with aspiring journalist Alison Chatterley. (978-1-63555-849-4)

Seasons for Change by KC Richardson. Love, laughter, and trust develop for Shawn and Morgan throughout the changing seasons of Lake Tahoe. (978-1-63555-882-1)

Summer Lovin' by Julie Cannon. Three different women, three exotic locations, one unforgettable summer. What do you think will happen? (978-1-63555-920-0)

Unbridled by D. Jackson Leigh. A visit to a local stable turns into more than riding lessons between a novel writer and an equestrian with a taste for power play. (978-1-63555-847-0)

VIP by Jackie D. In a town where relationships are forged and shattered by perception, sometimes even love can't change who you really are. (978-1-63555-908-8)

Yearning by Gun Brooke. The sleepy town of Dennamore has an irresistible pull on those who've moved away. The mystery Darian Benson and Samantha Pike uncover will change them forever, but the love they find along the way just might be the key to saving themselves. (978-1-63555-757-2)